"The story that plays out from here is more than competently told ... Toward the end of the tale a couple of questions I had about the telling are answered, so all of the loose ends are tied up, but in true noir fashion, not too happily for most of the participants."
—Steve Lewis, *Mystery*File*

"Tough and terrifying!"
—Richard S. Prather, creator of Shell Scott

# Awake and Die
# By Robert Ames

**Black Gat Books • Eureka California**

AWAKE AND DIE

Published by Black Gat Books
A division of Stark House Press
1315 H Street
Eureka, CA 95501, USA
griffinskye3@sbcglobal.net
www.starkhousepress.com

AWAKE AND DIE
Published by Gold Medal Books, New York, and copyright ©
1955 by Fawcett Publications, Inc.

All rights reserved under International and Pan-American
Copyright Conventions.

ISBN: 979-8-88601-014-5

Cover design by Jeff Vorzimmer, ¡caliente!design, Austin, Texas
Text design by Mark Shepard, shepgraphics.com
Cover art by Clark Hullings

PUBLISHER'S NOTE:
This is a work of fiction. Names, characters, places and
incidents are either the products of the author's imagination or
used fictionally, and any resemblance to actual persons, living
or dead, events or locales, is entirely coincidental.
Without limiting the rights under copyright reserved above, no
part of this publication may be reproduced, stored, or
introduced into a retrieval system or transmitted in any form
or by any means (electronic, mechanical, photocopying,
recording or otherwise) without the prior written permission of
both the copyright owner and the above publisher of the book.

First Stark House Press/Black Gat Edition: January 2023

## Chapter One

The day of the killing was one of the most beautiful I ever spent on the water. I didn't know murder was going to be done that night, and done by me. Because it was murder; I knew that then and I know it now. I knew just what I was doing, and that it was wrong. And I know that now. But I'd rather be called a cold blooded killer, have everyone say it, than that I was off in the head. Because I never was and I'm not now. I think clear and true, and this story would prove it if anyone saw it. Of course nobody will.

I did have something that hurt my head at times. In Korea, that last year of fighting, I got it in spite of the helmet. The helmet even made it worse, because the bullet drove a piece of it right into my head. The Army doctors said that was the worst part of it, and it took a second and then a third operation to get it all cleaned out.

Of course, in the end, they fixed me up all right. They fixed me up fine. First in Japan, and then in the vet hospital in New York. That was three years ago, though it seems like a hundred to me now.

They wanted to give me a 50-per-cent-disability pension. I laughed at them, but it angered, me. "I'm a Jersey clam digger," I told them. "They don't come tougher than that. I can still dig two tides a day. I wouldn't want people to think I'm only half a man. I'd be ashamed to take a pension."

Then they told me I'd have to report up there every two weeks to be checked, as there was no vet hospital near my place in Jersey. But I bucked that. The time I'd spent in hospitals already had nearly driven me crazy. I'm an outside man who'd die like an eagle if he had to live indoors.

It ended up by my getting my way. Below my town there's one called Bayhaven, on the rich part of the river. They told me I could report every two weeks to an Army Reserve doctor who practiced there and who sometimes helped them out at the vet hospital. His name was Dr. Algee.

I didn't know it then, but Bayhaven was where Claire Grace lived. If it hadn't been for Dr. Algee, I'd never have met her, would never have committed murder, and wouldn't be where I am today. But it wasn't his fault, and it wasn't Claire's fault. It wasn't anybody's fault, except fate's.

It had to be fate; because this day started like any other, except for one thing. After almost a year of Mae Hunt, I was at least my own man again. The night before we'd had it out. I'd taken all I could of her phony English accent, changing after one bottle to the lowest clam-digger talk; her drinking, her growing possessive attitude, and her increasingly sloppy dressing. From a once voluptuous, good-looking woman, she had degenerated to a nagging shrew who boldly announced she had got enough time in with me to make our relations legal in the eyes of the world. Those were her very words.

Nuts, I told her, I'm through as of now.

Yes, it started out as a beautiful day. I made a better than average haul. I got into a bed of hardshells that were thick as peanuts in a bag. The way you dig them is by shoving down into the water, then into the clam beds with a long rake. This rake has a bendy kind of pole, about twelve feet long with a crossbar on top. At the bottom end is a wide spread of tines, and they're curled up so that when you work the clams into their curve, you can lift the mess up without losing any, if you know your business.

This warm, sunny day, I loaded my baskets and the bottom of the boat. I didn't even feel tired, though it's the hardest work known to man. Because, over and over again, you have to fight those heavy tines down into the hard bottom, scrabble them around, drag it with its load all the way up. It's back-breaking work. And heartbreaking, when all you pull up time after time is mud and old shells.

But this day it was perfect. I could have picked the boat up with all its load and lifted it over my head. I felt that way. I felt stronger than I ever had in my life before, because I'd had it out with Mae and she was off my neck at last.

I was near the north shore, where the inlet is about a mile wide. I looked over my shoulder and there was Bayhaven shining like a hummingbird in the sun. All those private yachts and cruisers and speedboats, and behind them in the big trees were the beautiful houses where their owners lived. Bayhaven was the richest town in New Jersey.

I didn't envy any of them. There wasn't a man of them over there who could put in the three hours I'd just put in doing what I'd been doing. Or one who even looked more like a man than me. Put me in their clothes and you'd never guess. You'd think I owned one of those big yachts. I know, because people have told me so, urging me to get off the river and get a city job. Not me. I love the river. I was born there and I hoped to spend all my life there.

Anyway, this day I shoved the outboard down and went roaring across the river. Now, always before, I'd taken my clams to the upper bridge, to the Bridge Docks, and sold them to the fish dealers in town. They got three times as much as I did; but hell, that's the way the law of supply and demand works. I got enough out of it for my simple needs —that is, before they stopped being simple and I met Mae Hunt, who said "Gimme" all the time.

It must have been about eleven o'clock in the morning when I tied up at a clear space at the Bayhaven dock. I had no idea of selling the clams there; I just meant to take a basket to Dr. Algee, because he gave me my checkup every two weeks and never got any pay for it. And he loved clams. I was ashamed of that drunken daub *Mae* she'd painted on both sides of the bow of my boat, so I tied up in back, out of sight.

The tide was all right. The boat was only about five feet below the dock level. I caught the edge, chinned myself up, tied the painter, then dropped down into the boat for the clams. I hadn't seen her yet, but she'd seen me; because she left her easel and came over. She was looking down at me as I lifted that big basket of clams. It was a little tricky. I was on the bow thwart and I had to keep my balance, because a boat like that, even in still water, is always ready to move out from under you. If there'd been a man there, I'd have called to him, "Here, give me a hand." But you can't do that with a woman. Maybe with Mae, but not with one who looked the way this girl did.

I saw her eyes as I looked above the heaped clams in the basket. They were like big pieces of soft turquoise, the kind you see in rings. She had something tied around her head, but you could see the way the sun had gone to work on that blonde hair of hers. It was almost white. It would dazzle you, if you looked at it in the sun.

I had to take my eyes off her, or maybe go overboard. I was balancing on that tiny seat like a high-wire walker, and I had the basket of clams way over my head when I heard her voice: "Let me help you." No phony accent there. Clear, musical notes.

She squatted and reached out for the basket. I felt that high, light feeling in my head that sometimes happens. It's a mixture of being angry and proud, and very strong. "I don't need any help," I said. "Look out. Maybe some of them will drop and you'll get dirty."

I heaved them up then. I was bare to the waist, and I could feel the sun on my muscles. I knew how they looked because I've watched them in the mirror plenty of times. Mae asked me to do it a lot. A big lift, with all muscles bulging. And a basket like that was a big lift.

I set the clams on the dock like a bag of feathers, then hopped up after them. There were some people by the boats at the far end of the dock, but we were alone. I looked at her then. She was standing there looking at me, so why not?

She wore a white, half-sleeved shirt, opened well at the neck, and a pair of red shorts. Red always excites me, or has since the hospital. It scares me, too. Or maybe it was those long tanned legs. They were the best pair I'd ever seen. Mae was knocked-kneed and her thighs were as heavy as mine. She had a big front on her, but she massacred it with brassieres you could use for a horse's nose bag; that's what wine had done to her in a year. But not this one. Unless my eyes were off, she wore none at all.

Now she was talking to me, pleasantly and politely. "Do you sell those?" she said, pointing at the clams.

"They're a present," I said. "For Dr. Algee."

She smiled. "Oh," she said. "A grateful patient?"

I didn't like that. I'd never been sick a day in my life. A bullet in your head isn't being sick.

So now I said, "No." Why tell her my business? And I wanted to get away from her — from those red pants and those long tanned legs. I had to look at the easel, though. There was part of a picture on it, and I love pictures. I could look at picture magazines all night. I used to, until Mae broke into my activities.

This one was of the river and the boats out there; but there were no people in it. Maybe she guessed I was wondering about that, because she said, "Not much life there, is there?"

I pointed. "Plenty of live people at the end of the dock."

"The wrong kind of people, though." She smiled then and said, "But you with that basket of clams ... Would you let me sketch you in? It would only take a few minutes. I'll gladly pay you for your time."

If she hadn't said that about pay I might have done it. Who in hell did she think she was? Suppose I said to her, "Come on in my boat up to my shack, and take off those clothes. I'll be glad to pay you for your time."

"No, thanks," I said, and I lifted the clams to my shoulder. But, like all women, she wouldn't let well enough alone. If she had, there'd have been no murder; I might even have sunk back to Mae. She said, "Surely you're not going to walk way into town with that heavy load!"

"It isn't heavy to me," I said.

She was walking beside me. She said, "I'm awfully sorry about that mention of pay. I realize it offended you. Let's make it friendly: You pose a few minutes and I'll drive you to the doctor's. I have a car parked right by the yacht club."

Put that way, it was different. You don't like to hurt people's feelings when they're too dumb to know they've hurt yours. And it was a hell of a walk around to the edge of town where Dr. Algee lived. So I let her make the sketch of me and the clams, then put on my shirt, and she drove us to the doctor's. Nobody seemed to be home, so I left the clams in a shady spot on the back porch and covered the basket with some old newspapers I found out there.

During the ride she told me something about herself — not that I asked. I was surprised to learn that she was married. She said her husband was a businessman and commuted to New York. They lived at the end of Bayhaven away from Dr. Algee — that is, in the richer part, where the big estates were. She was in the money, all right. Her car was a red foreign-made convertible, and the engine moved like silk.

On the way back to the dock, she stopped in front of a place called Monte's Inn. It didn't look like a saloon. It was of gray stone with ivy all over it, almost like a church.

"What's this?" I said, and she said, smiling like a kid, "I thought you might like a Tom Collins. Monte makes wonderful ones, and today's hot enough."

Now, a funny thing: I'd a thousand times rather have had a candy bar. Dr. Algee told me they're far better for you, give you a lift that lasted, instead of the lousy way you feel after boozing. Candy and coffee, he told me. Not only your nerves and stomach, but booze was bad for your head, he said. Especially for me, until the inside of my wound really got muscled up. Three years wasn't time enough, he said. Give it a couple of more years and then we'd see about drinking. Well, it wasn't worth it to me to hold up that final healing and most likely be forced to go back to the hospital, so I just left booze alone. Mae tried to get me to drink. Right in front of me, night after night, she'd polish off a quart bottle of wine. It would excite hell out of her, make her love-crazy and sometimes mean. So there wasn't any need of my drinking it; she did it for both of us.

But now — hell, I could drink a Coke. A Coke would go good on a hot day like this. So we got out and went into the bar. It was dim and cool in there. There were a dozen or so red leather stools and an old, gray-headed fellow with a white coat on behind the shining bar. He didn't seem to think it funny, me in the old khaki shirt and dungarees with this swell-looking blonde. I found out afterward that even rich local boatmen tried to go about looking tough, to show they were working on their boats.

I never had the Coke. I'd mentioned it, but he put the two tall, white-topped drinks on the bar and I had to be polite. Hell, one drink with all that mix in it wouldn't hurt anybody. Even two wouldn't, because after the second one, I felt better than I had for years. And then she put some change in the jukebox and gave me an inviting smile. "Don't tell me you don't dance ... a man who can balance the way you can."

I didn't tell her, because I'm a good dancer. Light on my feet as a boxer. That's how I met Mae. I was in this cheap bar up back of my house, playing the miniature bowling game. Mae was on a bar stool, tapping her feet. She was slimmer and very sexy-looking at that time. She came over to watch me play and then said, "How about a dance, big fellow?" There was a sign up there that said, "Please do not dance." Something to do with the amusement tax, but nobody paid much attention to it.

I'd just made a strike on the machine and I felt good. So I danced with Mae. It seems she'd just had a run-in with this laundry driver she'd been tied up with, and she'd run him out. For good, and a lucky guy he was. Because I took Mae back to the shack that night, she liked the place, and she all but moved in. That I wouldn't have. No woman's taking over my little home. Not permanent. But there was no shaking her after that night.

Well, now I was dancing with this neat blonde and she was saying, "Will, you dance beautifully." It was that first time she'd called me by my first name, though she'd asked me what it was after the first drink.

I looked down at her, ducking my head back, because she was as close to me as you can get. "Mrs. Grace," I said, "how could I help it, with such a beautiful dancer as you?"

We both thought that was very funny and we laughed, and kept laughing. The old man behind the bar never looked up from the racing news he was reading. What a place! I thought. More privacy than in your own home. Mine, especially.

And then I got to thinking: Thank God that damned Mae won't be there when I get back, waiting for the clam money to buy wine. Lately she'd been drinking three bottles of the stuff a day, and been harder and harder to run out. Well, she was run out for good now. I kept comparing her with this Claire Grace. Here was the kind of woman a man ought to have. Why had I ever tied up to that bag Mae? Phony talk with the first bottle, mean fits after the second bottle, and never took no for an answer.

Mrs. Grace broke into my thoughts as if she'd been thinking right along with me. She was asking me where I lived, and how, and I told her. "I don't need much," I said, "but what I have is all right. It's only three rooms, but it's been worked over more than most big houses. It's warm and tight in the winter and cool in the summer, because it's right on the river. And you talk about pictures ... An artist like you would go for it. A high bank on my side and marsh on the other. Big trees where I am and you've got a million colors on the river — changing from daylight to dark. And no gabby neighbors — just a few other shacks, but away from me."

"Where do you eat?"

"I'm a good cook. I like to do it. And I keep the place neat as a pin."

That last was a lie, up to last night. But now, and before Mae came, it was true. Lately, after Mae'd been there five minutes, the place would look like a hog pen: cigarette butts all over, comic books, dirty glasses and bottles. It would take a marimba player to pick up fast enough after her, so at last I just said the hell with it, and let it go.

I realized finally, as I talked glowingly and more glowingly — because we'd had two more drinks — that what was way back in my mind was getting this Claire Grace up to my place. I was shivering with it. Her shirt had come more open, you could see half her breasts, and she didn't seem to care. I even had hold of her hand, and she squeezed mine. Married? That didn't make any difference. Even Mae claimed to be married. But hell, they'll all play. Or anyway, they will if they soap up to you the way this one had done with me.

I heard myself say it. "Why don't you come up and see?"

That seemed to hit the wrong bell. She sort of jumped and looked at her watch. "Gosh," she said, "I didn't realize it was so late. Know how long we've been in here?"

I didn't know and didn't care. It was late afternoon, the sun not coming in that one window any more. I began to sweat. I might never see her again. I had her warmed up now, and I might never get her back to feeling this way.

"Look," I said, "I've got a seven-horsepower motor on the boat. I can run you up there in less than half an hour. Right now, near sunset, you'll see the picture of your life."

I must have been breathing hard, or shaking, or

something, because she backed away a little. She tried to smile.

"I wish I could. It sounds wonderful. But some other time. I really have to run now. I'll drop you by the dock."

I had that feeling then, that funny feeling in my head. All she'd done was say a few words, but it was as if she'd slapped my face. I've got pride. I know a brush-off when I see it. But, damn her to hell, why had she led me on the way she did? Just killing time until her husband got home?

"No, thanks," I said. "I like it here."

She went through a few soft-soaping words, smiling all the time, pouting like a kid, but at last she was gone. It wasn't until I heard her car roar away that I knew. Right up to the end I'd thought she might come back.

## Chapter Two

It was good and dark when I went down the steep riverbank to my little house. I don't remember much of what went before. I know I was at several bars, but I didn't drink Tom Collinses. I never wanted to see another Tom Collins. But the funny thing: I sort of came to myself as I walked along the boards to my house. There was light shining out, so I could see. In one hand I had a square bottle of gin, and in the other a bottle of Tom Collins mix. My head felt funny, but I tried to think through it. I sort of remembered getting those bottles with the idea of smashing them. Maybe against the house, as a kind of ugly christening of the day I'd met, and then lost, Claire Grace.

Then it came to me: Why was the light on in there? Since Mae, I had to put on two extra locks. The old ones she had picked easy and I'd come back and find her there with that big mug going before I stepped in the door. But she couldn't pick those new locks. And last night I'd told her to stay away for good, hadn't I?

I had a wild feeling as I stopped and stared at the lighted window. An artist like Claire Grace might know ways. She had a tricky little sense of humor, too. Suppose — just suppose — she'd driven up here and let herself in? Suppose she was waiting for me in there, maybe had cleaned the place all up after Mae? Suppose she was waiting in there, sweetly smiling, and said, "I hated to leave you at Monte's, but I had to, Will. My husband is very jealous. But when I got home, he phoned from New York that he'd be away on business all night, so I came up to see your nice little place."

Just thinking that made me feverish. And, by the time I got to the door, I was sure that was what would happen. It was the back door, away from the river, and it was locked tight. I could hear the radio now, playing sentimental dance music. Well, she had to do something to pass the time, preserve the mood that had sent her here. She'd be eager to see me.

But she wasn't. She wasn't even there. But Mae was. She was sitting in my big Morris chair like the queen of all she surveyed. She was all dressed up and she was waving that long dime-store cigarette holder with the so called diamonds on it. Her brassy-dyed hair was all curled on top of her head, and she wore a glaring white makeup with bright-red lipstick.

She seemed to be only in her first stage of drunkenness, because she was using the phony English accent. Well, I was in my one and only stage of drunkenness: the first since I'd been wounded. I didn't realize that at the time. I just knew that all the ugliness in the world was boiling in me at the very sight of her. Last night I'd told her off. I hadn't been drunk and I hadn't been ugly. I'd put it coldly on the line and she'd seemed to accept it. Her boozing and the talk she was causing were more than I could take. Were more than I was *going* to take. I was putting new locks on the doors and I warned her I didn't want to find her hanging around.

"How did you get in here?" I almost yelled that at her as I snapped the radio off.

"Rahlly, dahling, you're becoming *coarse.*" She waved that damned holder, and the burning cigarette fell on the rug. I picked it up, mashed it out in a tray.

"I told you to keep away from here. How did you get in?"

"Now, Willie dahling, please don't play the wild boy with me."

She waved the holder and gave me that haughty smile. The funny thing, when I first met her I'd fallen for that English talk. She had it down to a T. She'd spread it around that her grandfather had been an English lord and her father had fallen on hard times in this country.

She said languidly, "Where have you *bean,* dahling? I've bean so rotten bored, waiting here."

"Nuts," I said.

I tried the front door, shaking it angrily. But that was locked, too. Then I realized how she'd done it. River wind came in from the bedroom. I looked in. She'd smashed the window out. I raved at her again. "That's vandalism. That's breaking and entering. You can be jugged for that, as well as for drunkenness."

She gave me the bored look, waved the holder. "*Jugged?* How *coarse!* One hardly can be accused of breaking and entering one's own home. *Can* one?"

I was really ugly now, standing there staring at her, feeling like hitting her.

"*Can* one?"

"Shut up!" I said. "And *get* up. And out of here. And stay out."

I knew then — a little, anyway — that it was remembering Claire Grace, and comparing her with this drunken babe, that so enraged me.

If she said, "*can* one?" once again, she'd be hit. But she didn't say it. She said, in that languid way, "You know, dahling, I've been browsing about a bit since I last saw you. Legal browsing. And I came upon some int'resting information. Cohabitation, it seems, isn't necessarily the transient matter you've conceived it. After a certain period it becomes not only respectable, but the basis for a more 'lasting union,' as the Constitution says."

"Get up and get going," I said.

She waved the holder, smiled that superior smile. "Not only that, but I find my Venus is in the ascendant."

The way she looked at me then, you'd have thought she'd won the Irish Sweepstakes. She lifted a water glass of wine from the table, tried hard to drink it in the new ladylike manner, couldn't make that, and dropped it in one piece down her throat. A few more of those and there'd be no getting her out of here. And she had a half-full bottle of that sherry yet to go. It seemed to draw her like a magnet; more so even than needling me. I noticed the haughty look drop off her face as she reached for it. Even she realized they couldn't go together. But the wine came first.

She poured another glassful, downed that. Now she was looking almost apologetic. I even felt sorry for her. I said, "By the bottom of that bottle, you'll be down to earth. Far from the jolly British Isles. So get on that boat and hurry."

Right then I must have thought it; I didn't realize it,

but I must have. She looked almost grateful, downed another glass of wine, and was right back in the old Jersey clam-digging mud. "Where've you been, sweet? I've been waiting and waiting and worrying and worrying."

"And breaking and breaking. Glass."

She flared up then, waved the bottle at me. She was tight as a drum now. "You think I'm so dumb I can't break glass? Or so unloving or undomesticated that I can't get into my little home? My horoscope said you didn't mean the nasty things you said to me last night. It said I should *act*. Oh, Will, where have you been?"

She'd never know where I'd been.

"Get out of here," I said. "Right back through that broken window. Your horoscope lied like hell."

All England left her then. All her phony airs. She called me a lot of dirty names, and I hate women who talk dirty. "Get out," I said. "And get out now. Or I'll throw you out."

Those dirty green eyes of hers were like a crazy alley cat's. "Get out?" she said. "That's not why I came in."

She started to whine then, and blubbery tears flopped down over her painted face. "See?" she said. She pointed to an old straw suitcase I hadn't noticed before. "There's all I have," she said. "That and you, lover. I was at Dillon's a while back — where I first saw you, remember? You were playing the pinball, remember? You were sweet that night, honey. I got to thinking about that tonight. How it made a new woman of me — a better woman. Reminded me I was born a lady."

"A better capacity, you mean. From one bottle to three."

"What have you got there?" she said, noticing the two bottles I'd put on the lamp table. Then she jumped up. "Oh," she said, "you sweet thing! Playing angry and brought me that lovely gift. Oh, lover, come kiss me!"

"Take the gin and get out," I said. "And from now on, stay away from here."

She looked at me funny. Then she began to blubber again. "Oh, my God!" she said. "Another woman! I know I know. Oh, lover, for God's sake, don't do that to me!"

"I never want to see another woman," I said. "Come on, get going."

"You're drunk. I never could make you drink. No man could. A woman did it. Some bitch has gone and done it. Oh, my God!"

I had all I wanted. Except one thing. That gin bottle seemed to light up, just beg to be opened. I had to have some of it. But not in front of her. I wouldn't give her the satisfaction.

I grabbed her suitcase. I opened the front door, which led to the little walk to the river. I had a small dock there, where I kept my two boats and a few others I let people tie up there. Maybe I knew right then what I was going to do — or why else would I have gone to the dock with her bag? Not just thrown it out the back door?

But I went to the river.

She grabbed my arm and hung on. "Beat it or I'll throw this in the river," I said. Back in my mind, as always, was the way of the tide. I have to keep a regular tide table in my head because of my business. You don't dig too many clams at high tide.

How it happened I've never been sure. But I think I dropped the suitcase, then got my fingers around her neck. It was black dark out there, the black river going fast toward the sea. I remember there were two splashes. One was the suitcase.

Later I was back in the house. There was a clock set

in the radio, and I looked at that. I was surprised it was so early. I'd thought it was near midnight, but it wasn't yet quite ten.

I reached for the gin, hesitated. I had to do some thinking here, but I couldn't quite seem to get hold of just what about. So I took one measured drink of gin, straight; and, sure enough, my head seemed to clear. Not only clear, but everything came back sharp and true. One thing stood out: I'd just murdered Mae Hunt. I knew she was dead when I tossed her into the river, because her head hung loose, away from her, like a broken duck's wing.

Now when the tide is going out, with the speed of the river added to it, at that deep narrow place, you've got action. Nothing stays where you drop it, not even if it sinks. Did that suitcase sink? I didn't know. Did Mae sink? I didn't know. But no matter — that tide would pull them both far away by morning.

When would they miss Mae? And who would miss her? I thought that out. She lived in a dump of a room not far from the clothing factory where she did some piecework. They had so many government orders that they'd take anyone on there, even in-and-outers like Mae. They probably wouldn't miss her if she didn't show up for a week. About the place where she roomed, I didn't know.

But the hell of it was, she'd been hanging around my place so long that someone would know it. Not that I ever took her out. There were several shacks near mine, within sight; but the people who lived in them were more or less like me: rivermen who didn't stick their noses in other people's business, and not overfriendly with cops. What worried me most was what Mae might have said about me to girls she worked with, or maybe some family she might have.

And then the sweat came out on me when I

remembered what she had said about being at Dillon's bar earlier that evening. Somebody saw her there, of course. She said she was moping, thinking of how she had met me. That meant she was well oiled at the time. No telling what she might have said. Coming down to see me, maybe. And that suitcase with her ...

My mind was working fast now. One thing was good insurance. An alibi. But how could I get one?

Then I remembered about my boat. It was still tied up to the dock at Bayhaven, unless someone had stolen it.

I jumped up. I knew what to do now. Bayhaven was almost ten miles away, and I couldn't use a taxi. I had to get there fast. I had to steal a car. Kids do it all the time for short joy rides, until the gas runs out. If you leave them quick enough, they're not missed until you're through with them.

I found one, a beat-up sedan, on a side street that led to the river. I ditched it three blocks from Dr. Algee's. I'd put on a different shirt, no wine on it, and I bought some chlorophyll in a drugstore, so Dr. Algee wouldn't know I'd been drinking. The only thing: Had he found the clams yet? If he had, my story wasn't too good.

But I got a break on that. The house was dark in back, no dog, so I got on the screened back porch without being spotted. The clams were just as I'd left them. But would he be home?

There was a bell button set in the doorframe, and I pushed it hard. I was in: A light went on in back, and the doctor himself came out. He snapped on the porch light and saw me. "Why, Will!" he said. "Something wrong?"

I'd rehearsed just what I was going to say, and I said it. "I've been way down to the bay," I said. "Got into a nice bed. I thought you'd like some." I showed him the clams. He wore glasses and he had to bend down as he peered at them. "They're beauties," he said. "I love them. Very thoughtful of you, Will. But isn't it late to be clamming? Can you do it in the dark?"

I was ready for that.

"Like a fool, I ran out of gas way down there; had to row for miles, and then walk way up to Sand Point to get it. I've been out since noon, but it was worth it. I've got a big boatload down at the Bayhaven Dock."

"Good. You must be tired. Come on in and I'll give you a snack and a cup of tea. Mrs. Algee's away for a couple of days and I'm batching."

That would be good, maybe make my alibi better. But I had to consider something else. This man was a doctor, and a good one. I might think the drinking I'd been doing didn't show, but if he did get wise, I might be worse off than ever. So I told him I had to get my clams to town before everything shut up. And when he asked me, peering at me through those thick glasses, how I felt, I said I'd never felt better in my life. Then he said, smiling, "Well, you can tell me all about it on your next visit."

At the dock, I hoped nobody had noticed my boat had been there all day. Luckily I'd tied it up in a backwash and the clams had been covered. I walked way out to the end, though, where the gas pumps were. There were lights on, some boat people about, and some kids fishing for whatever was there.

I talked to one of the gas men; told him I'd just come upriver with a load of clams, asked what chance there was of selling them locally. I got a good break. The man I asked didn't know, but a man standing nearby overheard and said, "What do you want for them?"

I told him my tale of running out of outboard fuel. It made me late for my normal market. To unload them all, I'd sell them cheap. I could see he was one of those sharp boys that you see around all docks where sporting boats tie up. Rich men troll for fish they can buy in the market for a fraction of the cost of running their big cruisers. They show them, have pictures taken, and then give them away. Or sell them to men like this one, cheap.

We made a quick deal. I'd registered my story in front of several witnesses, so then I roared wide open up the river. You might say, why this pin-point alibi unless Mae was found and the time of death decided to the minute? Well, these days they can tell that, pretty close. But the main thing I had to put over was that I hadn't been near my place since morning; that I was just getting back to an empty house. I had to have a witness for that. And I had to do something else: I had to get a line on Mae's doings and talk at Dillon's before she'd come to my house to stay.

About a mile below my place there's a big bridge, with a small boat-rental place close by. Just before I got up there, I did a little job of my outboard motor, so she conked out. I rowed in, told my story, and asked if I could tie up for the night. They knew me there, of course, and said sure. I tied the boat, locked the motor up, walked up the street, and cut right, and ten minutes later I entered Dillon's.

Dillon's was a cheap dump: beer ten cents, a shot thirty-five. Workingmen crowded the place until it closed at two. They were almost all locals and knew each other even if they didn't always like each other. There was a jukebox there and two pinball machines and a tough bartender named Jeff.

There were also, usually, some pretty tough babes that hung out there. I knew I could get one of them. I could get one they called Chris by just hinting I had a bottle of gin at my house. Or I could get a skinny one named Connie. But a woman would be bad to take there. If things went wrong, they'd say jealousy was the motive, me bringing another woman to the place. But I could use them another way: I could get them to talk.

So I got my usual Coke and played the bowling game. They all come over to watch sooner or later. When Chris came over I bet her a drink I'd make a big score I could have made but didn't. I bought her a boilermaker. Then I bought her another and she said, "You never used to be so generous, Will. Whyn't you have one yourself?"

"I never drink," I told her. "You know that."

"You're generous because Mae ain't here," she said. "She come back and ketch you, though, I don't want to be in the middle, or even on the edge."

"Come back?" I said. "Has she already been here?"

"She was watering her beer. Sad-sacking all over the dump. That moron Walter."

"Walter?"

"That laundry-truck jockey. Guy you took her away from. Her husband."

"I never took her away from anyone. You sure he's her husband?"

"Yeah. For real, not common-law. Like she says *you* are."

My heart sank at that. "She must be nuts," I said "Common-law, hell. There isn't any such thing."

"Yeah," she said. "Right. It's just a whore's alibi. But the suitcase and all; *you* know. It really gave the K.O. to that moron Walter."

"What do you mean? What suitcase?"

"Mae's suitcase. Eloping for true. Walter come in and tried to make up with her. She just give him the laugh. 'See the bag?' she says. 'That's my trousseau. So no use you deviling around my rooming house from now on. I've flew the coop'."

My heart jumped. "Flew it to where?" I said.

She gave me a coy look. "Now, Will! You great big handsome bum. Flew it for where any girl would like to roost." She pointed toward the door on the river side. One dark block, down the bank, and there was my house. That's what she was pointing at.

"Who heard all that?" I said, trying to keep calm.

"Just her and me and Walter. See, Walter was buying drinks like crazy over in that booth. Naturally I took advantage of it, her and me being together when he came in. But it was no soap. She jumps up sudden, grabs her bag, and beats it. But what burns me up was the insulting remark she throws out when she leaves. I won't use her exact words, but she sure proved she ain't the lady she's always bragging she is."

Well, things were different now. I'd intended to pick up one of the men I knew, a guy who liked to drink but not a lush, take him back to the house, and work on that bottle of gin with him. He could testify no one was there.

But now, no. This Chris knew too much. And she talked too much. But, as nearly as I could figure it, she was the only one who knew. She had been with Mae all the time she was in here — just she and this Walter. And they hadn't been sitting at the bar. She had pointed out a corner booth, far from the bar, where all the gab had been going on.

I had to take Chris home. Already she was beginning to talk too loud. But I had to do it carefully. She probably thought Mae was at my place right now; maybe had a key to it. If so, there'd be a light on, of course. And you could look down on the shack from the end of the street....

I said, "Chris, you like gin?"

"Love it. Love it, love it."

"Reason I ask is I just came upriver with a load of

clams." I told her the story I'd told Dr. Algee then, but added a little. "I ran out of gas and had to sell them at Bayhaven for peanuts about an hour ago. I even had to give some away, but a guy gave me a bottle of gin for a basket. I stashed it outside. I'll pick it up, you meet me down by the riverbank, and I'll make you a present of it."

The boilermakers had her pretty high by now. Her eyes were gleaming.

"*Meet* you there? Whyn't we go together?" Then she looked suddenly wise. "Oh, Mae! Some nosy here'll say we went out together."

"Mae, hell," I said. "I haven't seen Mae for days. But one of these nosies might tell your boy friend, and he might misunderstand."

"Ha-ha!" she said. "*Any* time! You never see me moping over some guy. I'd rather have a bottle of even lousy gin than Mr. America. What's keeping you, big man?"

Nothing, now. Now I was on my way. I gave her some change, told her to play the pinball machine, and eased out. I ran down to the house. It was just as I had left it. I got the bottle of gin, ran up the rickety steps to the bank. A few seconds later I saw her under the light in front of Dillon's. She came skipping along, the light behind her, and I noticed that her silhouette was slim, her figure not bad — yet. But nothing like Mrs. Grace's. Nothing at all.

She did it as though I'd told her just what to do. First she saw that I actually had the gin, then she looked down at the shack. She said, "Mae must be asleep. No lights on."

"Don't be dumb," I said. "The place has been locked up all day. And nobody but me has the keys. Nobody, now or ever."

"Oh," she said. "You don't have to get mad. Gee, it's a

crime you don't drink, Will. This bottle's nearly full. The guy must of just took one belt out of it."

One belt, I was thinking. That's all it would take. But this Chris wasn't a bad kid. She had a sort of pretty face — one of those turned-up noses, and her eyes were never mean. The whites of them were usually bloodshot, but the brown was still bright and clear. You don't like to hit a woman like that; not in the face, mess it up, make it ugly.

I hadn't thought out in advance what I'd done to Mae, but it had worked perfectly. I wouldn't have minded messing *her* face up — but Chris's I didn't want to. So it was best to do it just as I did with Mae.

## Chapter Three

Chris began ooh-ing and ah-ing when I let her in the shack and turned on the lights. It's not a bad place. There's a little screened porch in back, then the kitchen. I've always been proud of my kitchen, kept it clean and the shining things shined. There's a narrow hallway, blocked off from the kitchen by a swing door, and off that is the bathroom and the little bedroom. I dug the septic tank myself, got rid of the privy we used to have when the old man was alive. My mother? I never knew her; died when I was a kid.

But the best room was in front. It went clear across the house, and I'd put in an old store window I'd cut down so it framed all the river. I always liked nice furniture. I'd buy it at the Salvation Army and sand it down, polish it up so it was like new. But that damned Mae, she'd put up these lousy-looking plastic curtains, flowers and birds and fish and what-all on them, colored. And then she'd sewn a lot of crappy-looking covers over the chairs and the couch. Well, I could ditch them now and get back to normal.

Chris didn't let the scene interfere with getting that gin bottle open. She downed one as she walked around looking things over, and then she flopped on the couch with another and had her a cigarette. Those brown eyes of hers were still roving around and gleaming. "This is the nuts," she said, "the perfect nuts!"

"It's not bad when it's clean," I said.

"That Mae's a slut," she said. "She could of kept it clean in half an hour a day."

"If she was around," I said. "But that's exaggerated about her coming here much. Lately, anyway."

"You have a fight?"

"Nothing like that. We're just friends. But I don't like that talk about common-law and her moving in. That's wine for you. You suppose she told all that junk around? Or was it just to needle this Walter?"

She jerked her shoulders. "The hell with Mae," she said. "Whyn't you and me just forget her? And you have a gin. You do that and then I'll know."

"Know what?"

"Mae said she could never get you to take a drink at all."

Hell, I thought, Chris wants me to take a drink. It's little enough to do for her. I don't want her to turn sour on me, clam up. And it will be easier to do with liquor in me, the way it affects my head. So I took a drink and she liked that. Two more, and she said she liked me. "I always did, Will."

"I thought you didn't go for guys. I thought gin was your dish."

"I got the gin. And here I am with you, Will. Who'd of thunk it?"

Well, let her think it, if it made her last moments pleasant.

"Where do you live, Chris? With your family?"

I had to get a little data on her first. Who was going to miss *her?*

"Nah," she said. "Hell, they loused up enough of my life awready. Let's get on a pleasant subject."

The subject turned out to be the rapidly disappearing gin. I knew what she was leading up to: another bottle, before Dillon's closed. But she wasn't even going to finish this one....

I was using mix in mine and Chris was drinking hers straight. She was lushing up fast and she was getting amorous. She had no intention of leaving here tonight — I could see that. And she was showing lots of legs and everything else as she cat-squirmed every now and then on the couch, and rolled those bloodshot eyes at me.

"Why you sitting a mile away over there, hon?" she said. Her eyes looked dark and smoky.

I grinned at her and said, "You're dangerous."

"You're afraid Mae will barge in."

"Nothing like that. She just gave you a snow job. She's probably off with some other guy."

All of a sudden, as if a hot match had touched her, Chris sort of jumped and her voice came out like sharp bits of broken glass. "Damn her!" she said. "Just let her bust in here! I'll cold-cock that wino bitch!"

I'd been putting it off, I'd even been enjoying the gin and her string of gab. Because she didn't have a hard voice like Mae's. She *had* to talk soft — it was the way her throat was built.

Her throat. I looked at it. It was nice and round and soft. I'd have to mess *that* up. I didn't like to, but I had to. I looked at it this way: I was doing the deciding here. And who was more important to me — Chris, or me? I couldn't let her off now. That last explosion from her proved that. She'd *got* me to do something Mae never could — or anybody else, except Mrs. Grace:

take a drink. Take four drinks. You think she wouldn't tell that all over? She'd probably make it even better; say how she ran Mae and her trousseau suitcase out. "Cold-cocked her." That's the way it is with them when they drink; it takes some crazy form or other. Even me it affected. If I hadn't met that Mrs. Grace and then felt sorry for myself and ugly at her, and then hadn't drunk in those bars to drown my frustration, I never would have killed Mae. I'd been sore at her before, plenty sore. The time she hocked my twenty-two-dollar Cox reel and turned it into wine, I'd felt like slapping her silly. But I never laid a hand on her. I'm not the kind that can hurt a woman.

But now I could. Just as earlier, with this gin in me, I could do it. So what was I waiting for?

I got out of the Morris chair. Chris looked receptive, but I didn't move toward her. "You know what?" I said. I pointed to the gin bottle. It didn't have a full drink left in it. "I'm a funny guy. Always before I climb way up there to Dillon's to get a nice new bottle of gin, I go down to my dock and take a last look at the beautiful sky and the river."

She ate it up. "Oh, you sweet, gin-loving honey, you! I could love you to death!"

She came at me then and tried to. She kissed hell out of me. The funny thing is that I liked it. There was a hot nagging at me that said: You don't have to do it yet, you've got all night. Yes, all night, but then what? I might weaken. And what was one night? All my life was what I wanted. I had a lot of life ahead of me. I was only twenty-five. And Mrs. Grace had a lot of life ahead of her. This Chris, she didn't have any certainty of living from day to day. If bad booze didn't get her, bad car brakes would. She gave nothing to the world, not a thing. She couldn't paint a picture, like Mrs. Grace, or talk grammatically, or make some guy happy as hell with just a smile.

After that gin, while Chris was gabbing along, I was deep in my own thoughts. Let's face it, I said to myself. It's Mrs. Grace. Come hell or high water. She didn't brush me off. What in hell did I expect? A woman like that, she meets you and likes you, but she has to be careful. She can't go too far all at once. She draws back if you take advantage. She doesn't know you well enough. You might be a crook, or have a record. You might even be a murderer. You've got to put yourself in her place. It takes time. You can't do it all at once. Remember she has a husband. How does she know you won't go out and shoot your mouth off?

You've got to *win* a woman like that. You've got to be patient. You've got to see through her little acts, understand the promises in them. Like her sketching me in that picture. She wouldn't have done that with just some bum, any of those other clammers. And then the ride to the doctor's. And the invitation to have a drink. And paying for the drinks, even over my protest.

That didn't have to be a brush-off, what she had said. "I wish I could. It sounds wonderful." She could have meant that. At least she'd left the door open. And there was always the telephone book. But none of it would be any good if this Chris blabbed about Mae and that common-law suitcase. Or if that Walter did. I'd have to take care of him, too. I couldn't right now, because he wasn't here. But Chris was here.

I pulled away from her. I knew she'd follow me out to the dock. Follow me? Hang onto me like a leech and gab happily all the way. Gab about that gin I was going up to buy after a maudlin look at the sky and the river.

It was dark on the dock. The edge of the light from my front window didn't hit that far. And it was quiet except for a radio going in Old Man Masek's shack, next one downriver. There were no boats going by, nothing but that black sky, not quite as black as the fine of the tops of the wild, high river grass across the water.

She snuggled up to me, stumbling against me. "Ooh, it's cold out here! Put your arm around me, please honey. I'm cold."

She did it for me. She was softer than I'd thought. She had nice breasts under that plaid shirt she had on. Too bad. She had it all over Mae. Why Mae, then? Because Mae wasn't so bad when she first moved in on me. Before she got to the three bottles a day, she used to sew things up — she was good at that — and she could make the best snapper soup I ever tasted. And she used to laugh a lot, and I like women who laugh. She was really a good looker before she suddenly fell apart.

On the other hand, this Chris was a snob. She'd sit at Dillon's bar and wouldn't give you the time of day. She always put on a big act of being beholden to no man. Men who didn't know her would edge up, try to start a conversation. Or they'd have the bartender set a drink before her, hoping for an opening. But it never worked. She made a great play of paying for her own drinks. The man would find a return drink set up for him on the next round, but no conversation.

Chris would sit with a pile of bills and change in front of her at the bar. That was to show them she always paid her own way. She always seemed to have it. Some guy putting out alimony, I figured. Not that I cared. I never gave her a tumble. And until six months or so ago, I'd never seen her drunk. And then it was every night. But she'd stand up straight and try not to show it. And she'd never let a man take her home.

How I happened to get in her good graces was when these two hopped-up strangers tried to work on her at closing time one night. About a block up the street, they tried to force her into their car. I don't like to see a man mistreat a woman, so I beat both of them up, and Mae cut the first one I knocked down pretty bad with one of her shoes.

I made Mae take Chris home that night — a good way to get rid of her. Only for that night, though. Sick and tired as I was getting of her, she kept at me. But no more. That old woman of the sea was off my neck now for keeps.

But, here on the dark dock, I had another one on my neck.

How was that tide? That came to me with a jolt. Coming in, running against the outgoing river, it was always slow. I was still lucky: I had caught it just at the turn for Mae, and it runs for six hours. So I still had it my way — going out to sea.

Chris was clinging to me. Her words were drunken. "I'm looking for a star, honey. Star light, star bright, first star I see tonight ..."

She could look, but she wouldn't see one. Never again would she see one.

She was still gabbing like that when my fingers went around her neck. I did it softly; no quick jump at her. I just put them there affectionately. I felt that way about her. I didn't feel ugly, or sore, or hate her. I sort of liked her.

My fingers didn't shut the gabbling words off — not yet. Chris was fairly tall, and as her head went back a little I could see the shine of her eyes, even in the dark. Somehow they reminded me of that phosphorescence you see under your outboard motor in the dark of an early morning.

I got my legs around hers so as to hold her still. Women can kick like hell, and when they're mad or protecting themselves, their legs are stronger than most men's.

She made a sort of gurgling sound, and I thought, That's enough. No more talk. She might say some last thing that would make me feel bad later.

I've got hands, you wouldn't believe how strong. I've won lots of bets at bars squeezing things between my fingers — things the average man couldn't budge. Hours every day I have to work that crossbar on the clam rake, and it makes your fingers like steel. All I had to do was close those fingers real tight and there'd never be another sound from Chris.

But I didn't close them. It wasn't that I heard anything; it must have been the vibration. The boards at the inner end of my dock run up to the path. They're tight, but a man running on them would set up a vibration.

It must have been that, because if I'd waited until he yelled, it would have been too late. He'd have found a broken-necked woman in my arms.

He jumped at me like a madman, and he kept yelling, "What are you doing? What are you doing? Mae! Mae!"

He clawed and kicked at me, but I'd let Chris go by then and turned on him. He was just a blur there, and not a very big blur; and then he merged with another blur and it was Chris and she was cursing and whaling at him with her fists.

"You no-good sonofabitch," she said. "Don't you call *me* Mae!"

So that was it. So this was Walter. Sir Walter Raleigh arriving several hours late.

I put my arm around Chris, held her lovingly. "He hurt you?" I asked her.

"That louse? Don't make me laugh. Whyn't you throw him in the river, honey?"

She didn't sound as though she'd guessed. But how

could she help it? Hell, I'd had a strangle hold on her, even though I hadn't put the pressure on.

Well, find that out later. Now I had this Walter to deal with. The guy was crying now, and he was saying, "I didn't know, Mr. Peters. I couldn't help but think it was Mae. And I thought you was beating her up."

Chris turned on him then. "You ever hear of a man making love to a woman? A real man? To a real woman? They don't play patty-cake. A real man leaves a woman black and blue. Like you ought to be made right now."

That was one way to play it. But why get the man sore? He was as dangerous to me as Chris. Moping around like this, already looking for Mae, no telling what he'd say or do.

So I put my hand on his arm in a friendly way. "Look, Walter," I said. "This isn't the way for any of us to act. Chris here went off a little half cocked. You can't blame her, you breaking up our romancing on the dock here. Let's all forget it; go up to the house and have a drink. Get what's worrying you out of your system."

I gave Chris a warning nudge as I said this and she seemed sober enough to understand and agree. Or maybe it was just the mention of the drink. But I knew just what I was doing. I'd find out what this Walter had spilled around about Mae and me; and when Chris came back from Dillon's with that next bottle of gin, Walter would be gone. He'd be several hundred yards down that black river.

I knew Chris would pull the ladylike big act when I asked her to go for the gin. "What? In the middle of the night, unescorted? Where's your manners, Will? I ain't no cheap Mae Hunt running after wine."

So I beat her to that. I said, "Honey, I want to have a little private talk with Walter. I want to make him understand there's nothing between me and his wife."

Chris gave a graty laugh. "I can reassure him. He think I'd be drinking in a man's house at midnight if him and me wasn't awful close?"

Walter brightened up at that. "You mean you're shacking up here, Chris?"

She jumped at him then. "Shacking up! Will ought to hit you for calling his nice place a shack."

"I take it back right now," Walter said quickly, and he gulped.

He was a sad-looking guy: thin, scrawny; his faded brown eyes seemed to hang down on his pasty face. What Mae had ever seen in him beat me, because when she married him she was probably a good-looking girl. She'd never mentioned him to me much, and I only had a foggy idea she used to run around with him, among others.

I gave Chris the dough and she went for the gin. I knew she'd hit a few at the bar, and work on that bowling machine — she couldn't keep away from it — and want people to see she'd bought a new big bottle of gin. I could count on at least fifteen minutes.

When she left I gave Walter the one drink in the bottle, and then some wine still left in one of Mae's jugs. I let him sit down in my Morris chair. I had to find out fast whom he had told about Mae and her moving in with me for keeps. I put on a very pious act, digging that out.

I said, "Chris told me about what happened at Dillon's. It really shocked hell out of me, Walter. I've got a reputation to consider around here. My people lived here on the river for generations — all respectable, well-thought-of people. I had an uncle who was in the Legislature at Trenton, and a grandfather over in Asbury who was a judge. We don't play that way — my kind of people. You go spread a slander like that and it can be made a court matter.

You can be sued."

He gulped a couple of times, first looking guilty and then kind of defiant. And he said, "I don't come from no bums, either, Mr. Peters. My trouble's always been my intense pride. Mae, she give me many a heartache. But my pride kept me in self-control. Tonight wasn't the only time she's shamed me before outsiders. The three times she was picked up for intoxication I had to bail her out. Heartsick? Several of them nights I nearly did away with myself."

"You mean, then," I said, in an encouraging, friendly way, "you don't wash dirty linen in public? You'd have too much pride to talk about your legal wedded wife?"

"I'd be mortified," he said, and he gulped and his eyes got moist. "I got this asthma," he explained. "Here by the river don't do me no good. It was that started it. I'd go into it at night, cough and almost die with no air, and Mae would jest sit up and laugh herself sick. And it got worse and it takes your strength. You can't be real loving to a woman like Mae when you got the asthma. And her taunting you. You can't take that if you've got pride." He shook his head slowly, very sad, and then he said, "But a man like you — the river seems to make him stronger. And you make all that money, fifteen bucks a bushel on clams. Jest dig a basket and you got fifteen dollars."

Oh, yes, I was thinking. Just poke up a bushel in a few minutes and there's fifteen dollars. But for the retailer, not for me. Just while you're sucking a cigarette. No bad days. No snow in the winter, or heavy rain lashing at you. No boat jumping around under you like a drunken cork. No clam rake, which a guy like this Walter couldn't even lift, wearing your back and shoulders out. Oh, no, nothing like that.

But I controlled myself. I said, "How come, if you suspected me and Mae all this time, you just go off half cocked tonight?"

That was a fair question and one I wanted answered before he went off that dark dock. And I had to hurry him before Chris came back.

He kind of brightened up at my question. "A funny thing," he said. "You know, carrying laundry into a house ain't fun. Not for a man my build. Sometimes after doing that I'd gasp like one of them blowfish. I'd have a regular spasm. Well, a few weeks back I done that. I nearly fain'et right in that kitchen. The woman thrun water on me, then she brung her husband back, and turned out he was a doctor. Not only that, he was a real nice, human sort of a gentleman. So he took me in front, where he had a little doctor room. You know what he done? You wouldn't believe it. He made me hold out my arm after he listened to my heart. Then he pricked me with about a dozen needles. 'Watch this,' he says. I watched, and at one of them pricks up jumped a little red lump. 'There's the culprit,' he says. 'You got a ...' I forgot the word, but it's what give me the asthma."

"Was the word allergy?" I said.

He slapped his hand on his knee. "That's it! He give me a shot in the arm and a box of green pills. Mr. Peters, you wouldn't believe it. I didn't at first, thought it was my imagination. But after three weeks' treatment, them wheezes was gone, I could sleep like a baby at night, and I gained seven pounds and et like a horse. And, instead of firing me, like I knew was coming, they give me a two-dollar raise and put me steady on collections."

Well, well. Green pills and a needle. Made a man of him. Looking at him now, I wondered what he must have looked like before. "So then you go looking for Mae?" I said.

He looked eager. "I was ashamed before. She used to

insult me before other men — women, too — and deny I was her legal husband. But now I'm building up, she can't have that argument no more. So after a while tonight, I worked up my courage and come down here to have it out."

His eagerness, almost happiness, left him then, and I looked at the clock. Chris would be back soon now. I had to act fast. Now this guy was a man again, and that damned Chris had convinced him she had supplanted Mae, he'd be all over looking for Mae. He'd stir up hell, maybe even have the cops put out a missing-person report. And now he practically took the thoughts out of my head by saying in that whining voice, "Look, Mr. Peters, bygones are bygones as far as you and me is concerned. You been nice and understanding to me. And honest. So what you think? Mae just putting on an act, huh? She puts two and two together, huh? Just needling me about you, wanting me to coax her back? Me looking a hundred per cent better than she ever seen me, and you and Chris taking up like that ... It could add up, huh?"

It was a shame, that eager, hopeful look in his pasty face. Why not let him have that for his last thought? Hell, it's just as easy for you to let them die feeling good as bad. He was sitting there on the edge of the Morris chair now, holding that empty glass, jazzed up with his hope and the wine-gin mixture. I had to get him to that dock. I could do it here, right now while he was feeling that new life bubbling in him; but somehow I hated to see his face in the light when I did it.

I was just about to tell him: Why wait for Chris? She might be hours. And he needed a drink and I had some in the boat at the dock. Let's walk down there. I was thinking that when the big idea came to me. Two birds with one stone. I only have the two hands, and, strong as I am, I couldn't chance grabbing them both at once. No. I had a better idea. I had a foolproof idea. A honey. Because wasn't Chris living it up right now in Dillon's, on borrowed time?

## Chapter Four

I dug around in back, and from a bunch of empties I drained off enough for another wine for Walter, and a little later Chris came back high as a weather vane. She wasn't even nasty to Walter. After we'd made drinks, I got her alone in back and I said to her, "He's really a nice guy, Chris. Had a bum deal. I feel I owe him something. So you be nice to him. Leave a nice taste in his mouth."

"That may run into money," she said, "gin costing what it does. But what you say goes, honey."

It worked out fine. Chris figured she was in; she could afford to be nice to Walter.

We kept off the subject of Mae. We got to talking about past days on the river. We were all natives, and we knew about the same Jersey things — boats and clamming and crabbing and fishing and booze joints along the back roads.

After a while we put the radio on and danced. Chris hadn't wasted any time at the pinball machine, I could see. She's been at that bar. And Walter — after about three drinks from the new gin, you wouldn't think he'd ever heard of Mae.

That was the way I wanted it: Walter swelling with his new manhood and Chris working herself up with the gin and dancing. But not for me. I had other plans. I could tell almost to the minute when things would be ripe. Just about one more big slug for Chris ...

I didn't have to make it for her, even. She slopped it

into the glass herself, and I said to myself, that's the last drink the poor kid will ever have, so it might as well be a good one.

She flopped on the couch after that and I noticed Walter eying those white thighs under the snagged-up skirt. He wasn't thinking of Mae now. I'd guessed his trouble easily enough. Mae had been all he could hope for, drab as she'd become. And she'd be all he could get from here on, now that I was off her. But this Chris was younger and slimmer, and in the bars she'd kept men's hands off. Walter knew that. Add that and his new manhood and the gin and you had what I knew you'd have.

"Look, Walter," I said, "the kid's out for the night. She might as well be dead for the next ten, twelve hours. No point her lying uncomfortably there while you and me talk and drink. I got to hurry to get more gin before Dillon's closes. Be a good guy and put the kid in my bunk in the bedroom. Use my pajamas. Like you'd want someone to do for you if you were in that condition. As a favor to me."

All I needed was that ginned-up, excited look in his doggy eyes. As a favor to me? Oh, boy!

"Nothing I wouldn't do for you, Will," he said, almost choking over it. "Or for that little lady there. You both been swell to me. And that gin's on me." He dragged out a big roll of bills, but I waved it off, because he'd never drink any of that gin.

I wouldn't mind killing him now. It would be easier. The sonofabitch! Trying to make what he thought was my woman!

I couldn't miss now. I'd have to expect publicity, police and all, but only in a sympathetic way. Nobody could say it was my fault. But the best part of it would be that it would be over and settled right away. There'd be no worry and waiting, wondering when and if they'd find Mae's body, or when Chris and Walter might talk out of turn.

The perfect thing, what gave me the idea, was the revolver. That, and Mae's gab about it. One of the few times she even mentioned Walter was in connection with that revolver. Part of the time he made collections for the laundry, and he'd got a police permit and this cheap revolver. He never carried more than a few bucks, but Mae said it was to make him look big and important. He thought he'd lost it and had to report that, but Mae had taken it and tried to hock it for wine money. The loan people said no, unless she had a permit for it. Then she tried to get me to sell it for her. Not me. So there it was, had been for months, in the back of the drawer in the kitchen cupboard.

I got that, and a pair of cotton work gloves I used when it was cold on the river. I didn't need the light, so I snapped that off. In the front room I could hear the radio going, and I knew that Walter would be waiting for the back door to bang open before he lifted Chris, took her into my bedroom, undressed her as a favor to me, and then made a quick estimate of how long I'd be gone for the gin.

I fooled him. I banged the door, all right, and I even went out. I took a look around. The other shacks were dark; and, with that radio on, and as far as they were from me, they'd never hear that nickel-plated, cheap .32.

The window Mae had broken through was in the bedroom. I'd blocked it off for the time being with cardboard from a big carton. But I could hear through it, and I could edge it aside and see through it, or could have if there'd been any light. But it was dark. He'd closed the door.

He hadn't wasted any time, and that made me sore as hell. I could hear Chris mumbling drunkenly, saying, "honey, honey, honey." She thought it was me, and that made me sorer still. The sonofabitch!

I was standing on the box Mae had used to get in. I was shaking. I could hardly wait to slide in there and put that asthmatic bastard where he belonged. He was making funny little soothing sounds, more like a sick animal than like a man. I guess he was. I guessed he was taking Chris's clothes off, fast and furiously. But now was too soon. If I shot him now, the sound might bring her to before I could get a clean shot at her. Women can scream louder than any shot. A scream like that someone might hear and remember tomorrow.

So I waited. It was the hardest thing I ever did. Why, I can't figure. This Chris meant nothing to me. Mrs. Grace did. If I could have her, I'd let anyone shoot me the next day. I'd let this mopy Walter shoot me. It was really for Mrs. Grace I was doing this.

This that I was going to do now would help me with Mrs. Grace. It would be in all the local newspapers, maybe even in the New York ones. The clues could be easily read. A man and woman found shot to death in bed, the gun on the floor. Whose gun? Why, it was registered in the name of one of the deceased — Walter Hunt. Someone had shot him and his guilty partner with his own gun. Who? Well, his wife was missing. The records showed that once she had tried to hock that gun. And earlier that night she and the two cheating deceased had been talking it up in Dillon's bar. But what were they doing in Will Peter's house? Not his invited guests, obviously. What they'd probably done was got ginned up, broken into his house while he was away, and been caught at it by a vengeful wife, now on the lam. The broken window was there for anyone to see.

You couldn't get anything more perfect than that.

Mrs. Grace would read it in the papers. She was an adventurous sort, that was easy to see. And bored, having to kill time painting around the docks. She'd be tickled to death to ask me all about it, once I bumped into her again.

I've often wondered how it would all have worked out if it had gone as I planned. But it didn't. No more than with Chris, on the dark dock.

I went in there at last, and I shot Walter Hunt. I shot him twice, three times, to be sure. And each time the revolver fired perfectly, and he had it coming to him for what he meant to do to that drunken girl on the bed. Funny, she didn't let out a peep. She just lay there naked, as if she was dead.

But I had to make her really dead; so I shoved what was left of Walter Hunt away and put the muzzle of the gun close to her forehead, so she'd never know what had happened. So it would only be one gin drunk she never woke up from.

But the trigger spring broke. Maybe it was my strong fingers going ugly, like that. I had her cocked, but the trigger just slopped back loose. I'd heard about this "fanning" the old Westerners used to do. I tried that. But the hammer wouldn't fall.

I began to sweat. Hell, it had to be done with this revolver not some kitchen knife or club. Anyway, I couldn't use a thing like that. And if Mae was supposed to have done it the police would know she could never choke an active girl like Chris with her drunken hands.

What in hell was I going to do?

I'd simply have to settle for my original plan. No publicity. Just the opposite. I'd have to use my hands on Chris, then dump them both in the river. The main thing was to get Walter out of here first. Chris could wait. And not let any more of that blood get on the bed.

So I lifted her and she felt pleasantly heavy in my arms. I took her to the couch in the front room and put out the light. But I'd looked at her, and for the first time I realized what clothes do for a woman. They're supposed to improve them, hide their defects. Mostly they do. But they can do the opposite. You'd never have guessed, seeing Chris in jeans and shirt, or a cheap skirt like this and a blouse, how perfect she was beneath. Maybe almost as good as that Mrs. Grace. I hoped sometime I'd know for sure.

I pulled the shade over the broken window in the bedroom and looked the place over. Luckily, one of those plastic jobs of Mae's was over the bed for a spread. There wasn't much blood, and it was all on that. Plastic is non-porous, so there was no problem to washing that off fast.

I put the light out and picked Walter up. Pills or no pills, he didn't weigh as much as a bushel of clams.

I let him into the dark river gently, because I didn't want to make a splash. He went away with the current so fast he was out of sight in a second. Then I hurried back in, got the plastic spread, and tiptoed into the kitchen with it. I could have burned it, because that stuff goes up with a *pouf,* but it would mean lighting a fire on a summer night. Someone might see that.

I say a summer night; but that cold you get on the river around two A.M. had hit, and I shivered as I took that bloody, clammy spread out there. I closed the door carefully before I turned on the light. I didn't want the light waking Chris up, even if she *was* going down the river after I was through.

Funny about that — I could have dumped her in right after Walter. But somehow I hated the thought. The ungrateful bastard wasn't entitled to go down the river with her.

Easy as it seemed just to soap that blood off the spread, I knew a hasty job could be dangerous. It might look all off, but there were hems and seams and things that could hold maybe just a spot. In those laboratories they can pick it up through powerful glasses. I'd read that in many a crime magazine.

So I worked carefully. I went over that spread time and time again. I even used a big round reading glass the old man had left that was in the back of the cupboard drawer with all sorts of odds and ends. Then I at last hung the spread up so it would dry even. It ought to be dry by the time I was through with Chris.

And I had the revolver to think of. If I threw it in the river in front, that would be the first place they'd look for it, if anything went wrong. Or maybe dig up the yard. What in hell to do with it?

I lit a cigarette and thought that out.

A wind had come up, the before-dawn wind. I could hear the big trees by old Masek's shack grating and groaning away up in their tops. And I thought I heard another sound — voices. Maybe Chris was mumbling in there. So I'd better hurry; she might wake up, bare as she was, and that cold air coming in.

And then I guessed right. It was from over the bank. It was Dillon's two-o'clock closing. They were all piling out at once, and it was like distant surf on a breakwater. But some had to be pried out. Dillon's barkeep, Jeff, always had a job with the die-hards. Just one more drink.

I looked at the cheap, busted revolver. I could go on the porch, where my workbench was, and cut it with a hacksaw. I was thinking that when I jumped like a bee-stung cat. It shocked the hell out of me, that sharp rap-rap-rap at my back door. And then I caught hold of myself. You never know what a drunk will do. Chris could have waked up, gone wandering around out through the front door, lost herself in the dark.

So I stuck the revolver up under the sink plumbing and went to the door and opened it. I really got a shock then. There stood Rogers. And he was in uniform. Rogers is a mean cop, and full of his own importance. He'd been a detective once, but they'd demoted him, put him back on a beat. Something to do with a sharp deal he got into with a brother-in-law of his who ran a cigar store. He'd made himself the little king of the neighborhood and was cordially hated by all. They figured he was taking it out on them to make a record, get back as a detective.

He didn't like me. He never could get a drunk rap on me, as he had some of the others that went to Dillon's, but he was hoping I'd slip somehow, because of a remark I passed one night after his boasting. He was off duty at the time and I was squeezing bottle caps, showing off at the bar.

"Nothing to that," he said, and he squeezed a couple. Now, plenty of men can squeeze a bottle cap between their fingers, but try and get them to tear a telephone book. A big one. I did that just for the laugh, and it made him sore. There was only one book there and that made Jeff sore. So he had something to say, soaping up Rogers. "A mule can kick good, too," Jeff said, "but he can't graduate from the FBI school, top of his class, like Officer Rogers, here."

That's what Rogers had told all over about himself. He gave me that superior look. "Schools are for guys with brains," he said.

I said, "So that's why you missed that school in Korea — too many brains."

Everybody at the bar burst into a loud laugh. Many of the younger ones had fought in Korea, like me. And the older ones all swore they wished they could have qualified. But cops were deferred, and the talk was that Rogers had become a cop for no other reason.

So the guy didn't like me, and now here he was half in my kitchen doorway. My heart seemed dead. Fast work. Maybe he *had* stood high at that FBI school; and now he was having the last laugh.

My first thought was to ask him if he had a warrant. But that's dangerous. Right then you put yourself on the defensive, indicate you might have something to hide. And then I saw this big woman pushing in behind him. She had a hard, red face and a shawl over her gray hair. I'd never seen her before.

Both of them were in the kitchen before a word was said, and then Rogers said, "I'm here on a complaint, Peters."

I kept my voice calm, looked easy at him. "I do something out of line?"

"Where's Mrs. Mae Hunt?" Rogers said.

That sent my heart down as far as they go. I had to keep cool. I had to be sure not to give anything away by stuttering or talking too fast.

"Mrs. Mae Hunt?" I said. "How would I know?"

Rogers gave me a dirty look. "Mrs. Murphy here thinks you do know. She was up at Dillon's, and made her complaint to me. The woman rented a room from her over on Brock Street."

Mrs. Murphy's face had been getting redder and redder, and now she let go. "Yeah," she said. "Over a month back she owes me, and skips out sly as an eel while I'm at the supermarket. Bag and baggage. I just discovered it. I want my rent and pay for all the cigarette burns in my sheets and my nice veneer table she ruint."

I breathed again, but not very deeply. No foul play had been hinted at. I tried to keep cool, think out my next words, and I looked from one to the other, sort of puzzled. But then Rogers said, "This Hunt woman is a notorious bar fly, always at Dillon's, and you've been seen with her plenty, Peters. The inference is she came here."

It would have been cheap at double the price to pay this Murphy woman, rent, sheets, veneer table and all. But that way I'd be admitting a responsibility for Mae Hunt, and I couldn't afford to do that. So I said, "I can't see what this has got to do with me. I know Mae, yes, and so do a lot of other people." I almost added, "She's got a husband. Why don't you go to him?" But hell, I didn't want them looking for him, too.

Mrs. Murphy jumped in then, raging. "Oh, yeah? Well, Mr. Peters, me lad, says you! Irene Feeny helped Mae pack. She told me plenty. Like Mae told her plenty. And today was Mae's horoscope day. She read it out of the paper to Irene. 'Today is your day of decision,' it said. 'Make that big plunge you always wavered from up to now.' So she made that plunge, gypped me outa forty-six bucks, and shacked up in here with you, Mr. Peters, so mealy-mouthed you think you can kid *me!*"

With that she rumbled by me, and before I could stop her she pushed in the swing door and charged into the front room. By luck she found the switch just inside the door, and there she stood, staring at the stark-naked Chris, with me and Rogers right back of her.

"For cat's sake!" she said.

## Chapter Five

Rogers didn't say anything. He walked so softly you couldn't hear him, by me and Mrs. Murphy, and stood staring down at Chris. Then he said, very softly, "This woman isn't Mae Hunt."

Mrs. Murphy glared at me. *"She's* probably jest as nekkid in the other room. What kind of a pervert man are you, anyway?" she demanded of me.

I was wondering myself; but I didn't have to answer her because she shoved me aside and waddled fast into my bedroom.

Rogers was bending over Chris. "I know this woman," he said. He turned to me and his eyes were hard and mean. "That's Christine Humber, hangs out at Dillon's. Another bar fly."

Mrs. Murphy came back. "She ain't in *there*. But there's a window broke, so she must of heard us come in and jumped right through it."

I suddenly felt mad. Maybe it was because that cop was putting his big dirty hands on Chris, pretending to feel for her heartbeat. I gave Mrs. Murphy a blast. "You old bitch, you," I said. "Get out of here. There's nobody you know here, and there hasn't been. Go look somewhere else. Or I'll ask that you be arrested, barging in here without a warrant. I don't have to take this."

I looked at Rogers then. He jerked his hand away from Chris, and I figured: Now I've done it. I'd lost my head and the next thing would be a pinch.

But I guessed wrong. His voice wasn't hard when he spoke; it was almost friendly. "What you got to say about this girl being here, Peters?"

"Only just what happened. A while back she came here with a bottle of gin. I don't drink and she put most of it away. Then she passed out on me. I couldn't throw her out."

"Oh, yeah!" Mrs. Murphy chimed in. "She had to get herself stark nekkid to drink a little gin? So it would be cooler this nice hot night? Crap!"

Rogers waved a hand at her, then looked at me carefully. "I could take you in for this, Peters. It's a statutory offense. It could be even worse if this girl's a minor, like I suspect. You know that."

I had my wits back again. I tried to look the way Walter had looked when he thanked me earlier. "Yes, I know that," I said. "It looks bad. But it's really what I said. Nothing wrong between us."

He gave me a raised-eye brow look. "The *real* thing you said was: no search warrant. I never make a pinch unless the evidence will hold up in court. You might beat this on a technicality."

"Like hell he could," Mrs. Murphy burst in. "Ain't I a reliable witness? Can't I swear I seen this shameful sight right with my own two eyes? This dirty slut layin' here nekkid as a jay bird, waitin' for her turn after he slaked his passion on that bag Mae Hunt, who jumped out the winder oncet she heard my voice? Taking the spread to cover her sloppy nekkidness?"

"That's all speculation," the cop said. "The spread's in the kitchen. Wasn't that it hanging there, Peters?"

"Yes. The kid got sick on it."

"My forty-six bucks ain't speculation," Mrs. Murphy said. "By God, I'm going to get that or go to Judge Martinello as soon as the sun rises."

So I had to do it. I gave the cop a look that I hoped explained it. I said, "I don't want this innocent girl messed up in a scandal. It's worth fifty dollars to me not to have that, Mrs. Murphy. But just remember his: It's because you've had a bad deal. But I haven't seen Mae Hunt for over a week, and I'm not responsible for her in any way."

The money did it instantly. She was all smiles as she grabbed that dough and stuck it in a huge handbag. Then she went clucking around, motherly as hell, tucking Chris up with a blanket she found in the bedroom.

But the cop stopped her. "This girl can't stay here,"

he said. "That would be compounding a — a misdemeanor, anyway. Get some hot coffee into her. And get her clothes on. Where does she live, Peters?"

"I haven't any idea."

But the dressing and the coffee brought Chris out of it. Not much, but enough for her to realize the spot she was in. When she saw the cop, she was really scared. But, like all those girls who frequent bars, she knew enough to keep her mouth shut. I got in enough explanation so she knew the story, and then she backed me up. "Will's not to blame," she told Rogers. "A guy was bothering me at Dillon's, so I came here to drink. I must of pulled my clothes off in my sleep."

Rogers appeared willing to let it go at that, but I didn't trust him. He had a speculative look in his mean eyes. And when Mrs. Murphy helped Chris walk away, saying she'd drive her home in her car, the cop lingered a minute. His eyes never stopped going over the place, but his voice was easy enough when he said to me:

"A word of friendly warning to you, Peters. Bring lushes like that girl, or Mae Hunt, into your house and it begets real trouble in the end. You get a husband or a father down here looking for them with a gun and you've got only yourself to thank. I'm no circuit judge, but I've got plenty of authority in this neighborhood. So I'm saying to you now, lay off that Humber girl. I'll pick you up if I see you with her again. That Mae's a grown woman, but this Chris is something else again."

I don't know why, but something in his voice and in his eyes told me there was a lot more than friendly warning behind those words. I'd seen the greedy look he'd given Chris on the couch. I admit I'd never have guessed, seeing her around, dressed up, that she could be as smooth and as softly white-skinned as he was.

If it wasn't for Mrs. Grace, if I'd never seen her, Chris might have had the same effect on me.

Well, he could have her. I'd stay away. I'd stay away so hard maybe this mean cop would come to like me. So I said to him, really sincerely, "I give you my word she don't mean a thing to me. Like you say, she's just a kid. And a nice kid, too, as far as I know. Thanks for everything, and I'll remember what you said. Because you are as right as rain."

He gave me a little nod and backed out, and I watched him stride up the hill, big and eager.

I didn't sleep badly that night. I just said to myself, Tomorrow is another day. Start from there. With a clear head. So I got up about eight, made me a damn good breakfast of orange juice, bacon and eggs, toast, and coffee, sat down with a pipe, and thought everything out. Then I got up and went into action.

First that cheap revolver. I used my big hack saw and cut it up and threw the bits into the river.

Next came Old Man Masek. I'd wave to him from the boat, as you do to everyone passing up or down the river, but I'd never once gone into his shack. As for calling on him, just once had been enough for me. It embarrassed me; though, in my opinion, a man's entitled to his peculiarities.

This Masek had a real funny one. Every day about nine, he'd carry a big chair with the stuffing sticking out from his shack as if he was carrying a sick baby. He'd set the chair in the same spot under a big oak tree and take five for the day. The only moves I ever saw him make were when he reached down for another can of beer, opened it, and went to it. His bare feet were white as a fish belly, with enormous, twisted big toes.

But that wasn't the peculiar part. He had this funny looking dog and a cat, and right off the riverbank there was a fallen tree branch. Just as sure as the sun rose or set, this mangy old gray sea gull would sit on it. Stay there from sunup to dark.

But that still wasn't the peculiar part. You wouldn't believe that, unless you saw it and heard it. Masek never said anything to you himself; he'd have those animals talking it. If you said, "Do you know what time it is, Mr. Masek?" he'd turn to one of them and put on their voice in answer. Say it was the sea gull; maybe the sea gull would answer. "Hell, no! Time was made for slaves."

The sea gull — he called it Wilbur — was supposed to be the tough one, and pessimistic, with a foghorn voice. The dog spoke with a thick hillbilly accent, and the cat in mincy tones, very ladylike. He'd have the sea gull get in a profane or obscene word, and the dog would make a Southern gentleman's objection because of the cat's presence. Apparently when they were alone, all sorts of matters were discussed and debated.

I had one now that had to be settled. So I got some cans of beer from Dillon's and went over and dropped them, cold, at Masek's feet. I was careful to say good morning to the three animals, and let them note that I also had something for them.

Masek didn't give me one look, but the dog thanked me. The dog said, "We sure do thank you, Mr. Peters. Y'all hu'y back."

Masek opened a beer can and swallowed from it with relish.

"I wonder if any of you fellows heard a prowler around my dock last night. I found one of my boats tampered with this morning," I said.

"Sonofabitch," the sea gull said. "I hope you winged him. I thought I heard some shots."

That's what I was afraid of — that broken window, on Masek's side.

"Ah think Ah heard someone nosin' aroun', too," the dog said.

"Me, too," the cat said in that prissy voice.

For God's sake, I thought. Have I got to get it from these damned animals? Can't the bastard talk? With six cans of cold beer to spur him on?

I said, "That wasn't shots you heard, Wilbur. Maybe the door slamming. But you would have, if I'd had a gun."

"Y'all was in the war, so why don' you have a gun?" the dog said.

"I'm sceered of a gun," the cat said.

Hell, I was wasting my time here. But I could tell from Masek's pale-blue eyes that the beer had made him happy. I'd said there'd been no shots. I felt hopeful that if Rogers came nosing over here with any questions, the animals would stick up for me. I tossed some opened clams to Wilbur, a bait fish to Phoebe, the cat, and a forty-cent pork chop to Arthur, the dog. Even at a murder trial, a jury would hardly convict you on a sea gull's testimony.

So I left there.

Now what about Chris? I'd tipped her to the story that she had called on me uninvited with the gin, but I'd had to say it in front of Rogers and Mrs. Murphy, as though I were just explaining her befuddlement at being in my place. I hadn't dared or had a chance to tip her off about the vital thing: the lie that we'd been alone all the time. No Walter. And I was worried.

I was worried because it wasn't until the cop left that I realized there were three empty glasses in the front room. Rogers might or might not have noticed that. He had noted the spread in the kitchen.

I had no way of contacting Chris except at Dillon's. And she wouldn't be there until night. Or maybe she'd be afraid to go there after what had happened, knowing it was on Rogers' beat.

I couldn't just sit there and sweat. I have to have action when I'm upset. So I walked down to the bridge dock for my boat. I guess I must have known subconsciously, but I would never have admitted it. Because I did what I never do. Clamming, I wear Army fatigue pants and any old kind of shirt or sweater. But this day I put on clean khaki pants and a striped jersey Mae probably stole somewhere and gave me last Christmas. It made me look big and muscular, my arms bulging out below the short sleeves.

It was a nice sunny morning, hardly a ripple on the water, and the snappers were bait-jumping. I had a rod in the boat and a feathered jig. So I trolled down toward the inlet. They'd been catching big blues and a few stripers in the upper river, so nobody'd guess I was going that slow way by Bayhaven looking for a woman in a white blouse and red shorts.

But that's what I was doing. I couldn't help it. I had to see Mrs. Grace, if only just to look at her from the boat. Because everything I'd done was on account of her.

I picked up five snappers before I came close to Bayhaven. Try to get them to hit and you can't. Now they were bothering hell out of me, hitting one right after the other, keeping my eyes off that dock, getting closer and closer.

Then, when I was almost up to it, a striper hit. On that light rig it was like a pile driver. It's a thrill you rarely get. I've known men to troll for months and not get a striper hit.

I snapped my engine into neutral and I had to give him drag. He'd bend that light rod till the tip hit the water, then she'd go slack and I thought I'd lost him. But he was coming to me, and I had to reel like hell to keep him from jumping and throwing that light hook.

I wasn't noticing where I was. In a case like that you don't give a damn where you are. It was an out tide and he'd moved off to the land side, was pulling the boat. I knew what he was doing: making a run for those piles of the dock. If he got in there, with my line twisted around the piles, the barnacles would saw it quick.

I stopped that. I really set up on him, line or no line. Let it break. It fooled him. He didn't know how light it was. He came to me with a rush and I reeled like hell. I felt the boat bump, but the hell with that. I saw him now, green and silver. I had him close to the boat, but with that rig I couldn't horse him in. He was too big. I had no landing net or gaff. So I grabbed my clam rake and held it near the lower end, just like a net. Try that sometime. It's like using a kitchen stove with one hand to scoop up firewood.

I could hear them on the dock now, a gang of kibitzers, all giving advice and calling to others and betting on what and how big it was, and that I didn't have a chance of boating him.

I fooled them. I forked that big bastard into the boat and he barely fitted in the swell of that big rake and he was longer than that.

Well, when I came up for air, there I was, right against a dock pile in between two big white cruisers. The people on the cruisers and on the dock were all gaping down at me, yapping and praising me and saying, "Bring him up and weigh him. I bet he goes over fifty pounds."

Well, there was my chance to go up on that dock with a good excuse. But, by the same token, it was the worst thing that could happen if she was up there painting. All eyes would be on me and that striper, and I wouldn't dare talk to her.

But she wasn't there. The angle guy — the guy who hung around for easy bits, who'd bought my clams at half price the day before — he was there. He was right there and he wanted to buy that fish for another song. You try to buy a striper in the market. If you can get it, it will run you almost as much a pound as sirloin steak. This I had was, just for meat, a twenty-dollar job. I'd get that, later on; I wasn't taking the seven-fifty this guy kept nudging me for.

I gave a good look over the dock. She wasn't there, so the hell with it. I'd take the striper back to Snyder's market and get back part of the money I'd given Mrs. Murphy.

Remembering her gave me an idea. Last night she'd taken Chris home, very lovingly and motherly. She'd know where I could get in touch with her, and she'd have a phone. On Brook Street she lived, the cop had said.

I brushed the angle boy off, and I was going back down into the boat with the fish when this guy with a yachting cap stepped off a white cruiser tied up at the dock. He had a tall glass in his hand, looked like a highball. Pretty early in the morning for that, but those people are at it all day.

This man had a good tan on and didn't look too potbellied or soft, like most of them. He stared at the striper admiringly and asked me a few questions. On the deck of the cruiser, his men and women friends were gawking at the striper.

What he wanted to know was what the striper had hit on. "We're going downriver and then outside and troll along the coast. Might as well know what they like before we start."

I showed him the little jig, but told him it was only luck I'd made it with such light tackle. While I was talking, a pair of them from the cruiser joined us. The man had his arm around a blondined babe, who was already drunk and advertising the fact with all sorts of wisecracks.

"What do *you* care?" she said to the man. "You'll be three sheets to the wind and seven seas over by the time we pass the Hook. Fish are for the birds — the sea gulls, Dixon."

"That gives me an idea," the man said. "What will that fish sell for, Mac?" he said to me.

I didn't like his condescending manner or his red, ugly face, or that highball he also had in his hand, so I said indifferently, "Fifty bucks, Mac."

The first man shoved a five-dollar bill in my hand, thanked me and said, "Come on, Dix, we've got to consider the tide."

"Yeah, it waits for no man," the woman said.

"It waits for *me*," her boy friend said. "And that's not all that will be waiting for me. I've got to have something to show her for the day." He hauled out a big wallet, peeled off five tens, handed them down to me, and took the fish. Why I let him do it, I don't know, I don't know. Maybe a premonition. Or maybe those bright new tens — brighter than the ones I'd given Mrs. Murphy.

But I didn't say thanks. I fooled him on that. And when they took off in that cruiser, I watched them go. The name on the stern, in gold, was *Calypso*.

To hell with them.

I got into my boat and boiled upriver. Waved to Old Man Masek and his panel forum as I went by, tied up at my dock, and walked up to a pay station to phone Mrs. Murphy. She wasn't at the supermarket; probably sticking close to see that no more of her roomers pulled a Mae Hunt. She was sweet as pie to me when I told her that Chris had forgotten a package at my house, and did she know how to get in touch with her? She did and I called Chris, got her out of bed. She had an awful head and she was worried, but talked very lovingly to me. She wanted to meet me, even after I reminded her what the cop had said. "We could have just a couple of whisky sours at the Bridge Inn. He wouldn't see us there."

"But somebody else might, and gab. The main thing is, if he checks on you, nobody else was at my place, just you and me."

"But what about Walter? You mean him?"

"Just who I mean. He left when you passed out. After making some very critical remarks. Can't hold his liquor."

"But how did I get disrobed like that?"

"You must have disrobed yourself in your sleep, when I was gone."

"But that Walter? I hope and pray he didn't see me like that."

"No, he went when I did. I left him in front of Dillon's. He had to get up early for work."

"That makes me feel better. Mrs. Murphy turned out lovely. Like a mother, riding me home like that. She won't say anything. But that Rogers?"

"Cops don't talk about those things."

"But I have to see you, honey. You know how I feel about you now. Especially after last night."

"What do you mean by that?"

Her voice got low and silky. "You know. I can't discuss that over a public phone, sweet. When?"

"Wait a day or two. I'll call you. All right?"

She sighed. "If it has to be that way, honey. You know best."

I hung up. Well, that was done. I left the pay booth and went over the morning papers they had at the railroad newsstand. No word of any bodies being found in the river. So now I could go home, make a nice lunch, and listen to the one-o'clock news on the radio.

But I didn't do that. I did just what I must have known I'd do all along. Something I swore I wouldn't do. I told myself I was just looking in the phone book to see if she was there. There was only one Grace listed in Bayhaven, but they had three phones; one for the gardener's house, one for the stables, and one for the main house. That was unusual enough, but nothing to something else I noticed. Maybe I was wrong, and it was just one of those odd coincidences. Still, funny things happen. One happened when I got home.

Mrs. Grace was on my dock, just about to leave because no one had answered the door.

## Chapter Six

My heart seemed to stop for good when I saw her. In the sun there on my little front porch, she looked like an angel. She looked like an angel in a red blouse and slinky blue slacks. She didn't have the bandanna on her golden hair now; it was hanging heavy and curling almost down to her shoulders. And her blue eyes were shining like water splashes in the sun.

She was glad to see me. Her teeth gleamed in a happy smile. "I was just about to leave. Gosh, this *is* a jewel of a place isn't it?"

"How'd you find it, for heaven's sake?" I sounded silly even to myself.

She laughed. "What a picture!" she said. She waved over the high reeds that almost hid the place. From here, nobody could see us, not even Masek.

"How'd you get here? I didn't see your car." I waved up toward the bank.

Her eyes crinkled as she enjoyed watching my

bewilderment. Then she pointed to the dock. I saw it tied up between my two sad-looking boats. It was a beauty: bright red with a white arrow at the bow. It was maybe twenty feet, a cabin in front, with a high-powered engine in the cockpit. Those boats will do twenty miles an hour.

"Aren't you going to ask me in?"

I was shaking so I could hardly get the key in the lock. Then I saw the package she was pointing out for me to pick up, set by the door. She winked as she saw me watching. "Greek girl bringing gifts," she said.

Inside it was cool and pleasantly dim because, before I'd left, I'd pulled the Venetian blinds all down. "My, this is heavenly!" she said. "We might be out in Tahiti or somewhere. May I look around while you do the honors?" She added, "I'm parched, really. It's early, but this is an occasion. A glad-to-see-you-aboard job. Or are you. Will?"

"I'm delighted," I said. I didn't tell her I'd never thought she'd do it. Or that maybe she'd pretend she never saw me before if I met her somewhere. Be humble with women like that, or overly grateful, and you lose ground fast. The thing to do is take them in stride, just as if you expected them to act as they're acting. Be humble inside if you want, grateful as hell, thank your lucky stars, as I was doing then — but don't show it.

In the package were two bottles of good gin, four bottles of Tom Collins mix, and some lemons. And there were two big bottles of champagne. Just looking at the champagne scared me. I'd never tasted it in my life; didn't even know how to open it.

While I was unpacking the stuff, she came into the kitchen, looked that over, and said, "Why, it's as neat and snug as a Pullman kitchen. Will, you do yourself well, don't you?"

"It's all I have."

She was looking in my refrigerator. "Got a bucket?" I handed her one. She had the ice trays out of the box. "I think there's just about enough of these to cool one of those bottles. And by that time there should be some more ice."

I had my back to her, making the drinks. My hands were still shaking. But one thing I knew: never again! No more booze for me. All the killing I needed to do was done. And drinking doesn't mean fun to me. Not since my head was hurt. So I made hers a big one, lots of gin; but mine was just the mix. You couldn't tell the difference. She just glanced in the bedroom, taking no chances on walking in there and maybe having the suggestiveness of it stir me up. She was being nice, but under it all I could sense that she wasn't sure. I could spoil everything by getting too personal with her. Go too fast now, or show any indication of it for the future, and I could ruin everything. Anyway, in a case like this, it doesn't matter what the man wants, or how bad he wants it. The woman decides. Deep in herself she makes the vital decision. This business of seduction is overrated. Women aren't seduced by men; they're seduced by themselves. Just give them enough rope. If they don't want to use it, there isn't a damned thing you can do. So, if you watch yourself, you can at least come out of it with your self-respect. You can say: So what? I never even tried.

So I put up the Venetian blind on the river side and we sat and looked out, sipping at our drinks. Suddenly she laughed gaily. "You were right about the color here, Will. Just look what that window frames! But what I was laughing at was that old beachcomber next door. Good grief, that thing he lives in is just a piano box! Or does he live in it? It's like one of those cartoons — you know, the old hillbilly family with Paw in the grass-grown swing. And that overstuffed chair — out of this world!"

I didn't like this. "You were over talking to Old Man Masek?"

She laughed again. "They didn't tell me his name. That frowzy sea gull did most of the talking. He was the first person I saw above the bridge, so I slowed and called out. I asked where you lived."

"And Wilbur told you?"

She said, "Wilbur? That the sea gull?"

"So I hear. Did the cat or dog say anything?"

"One of them did. Just chimed in, sort of *sotto voce*. That all you've got for company around here?"

"I've got you now," I said. "How did you happen to come up?"

She looked down at her drink and frowned. I guessed she was debating whether to lie or tell the truth. At last she said, "Weekends, my husband goes fishing-crazy. I don't go any more, because I just couldn't take it. Two days a week and half the night wallowing around out there trolling. I didn't mind that so much, but the gang they always have to have along. It's really just one big booze party; the boat jammed with free loaders. It's really dangerous, too. Because they effect an amateur crew. Get a boat just big enough to handle without paid help. That way they can raise all hell out there and no one to talk about it later."

"How do you mean, dangerous?" I said.

"Careless handling. Once we rammed a dragger in the fog. Another time we ran down a crabbing boat downriver and killed a man. It cost plenty to pay that suit off. That was enough for me. I got this boat outside, and just go around the river. They can have their ocean."

I smiled at her, she was so intense, and I said, "What's your husband's first name?"

She answered before she thought. "Dixon," she said. Then her eyebrows went up. "Why?" she said.

It wasn't time to tell her why yet; it might never be. I'd have to see how those drinks worked on her. So I said, "Just curious."

"Be curious and see how the champagne is coming?" She smiled at me.

I went out and turned the bottle around in the bucket. I made her another strong Tom Collins, because the champagne didn't seem very cold to me. I wasn't trying to get her drunk. I knew as I made those drinks that I loved this woman. I loved her.

I might not have actually loved her if she'd left it as it had been. But her coming here did it. Proved something. All I wanted was to break down that difference between us. That social difference. Drink could do that, if deep in her she was attracted to me. I thought she was; her coming here was a sort of proof. I'd settle for just looking at her. Even without that soft, sort of gurgling voice, without a word out of her, I'd be happy. Just an hour a day, even. Because, even when she was silent, she sort of talked to you with those warm blue eyes.

She did that when I brought the drink back. And, as she sipped at it, she asked me all about myself. You couldn't fool a woman like that, so I told her the truth and she seemed to like it. I even told her about the head wound, and I didn't mind a bit when she said, "Poor boy! Let me look at it."

Her drink was gone then, and I think she was feeling them. Because when I went to her, bent over so she could see the dent in my head, her fingers went up there, and they weren't just feeling, they were caressing.

I did something I had never done before: I took her fingers and kissed them. She drew them slowly away and looked up at me with those blue eyes, very soft now. It was a long look that made me turn almost inside out. But I knew enough to get away from her, and to say pleasantly, "That champagne ought to be cold now."

"Good," she said.

She jumped up then. Maybe she guessed I didn't know how to open the bottle, because she went with me to the kitchen and did it herself. When she was bending over for it, I put my hand just a second on that golden hair, and she smiled up at me. She wasn't sore yet....

She found some sherbet glasses Mae had won on a punchboard, and she poured the stuff into them. I couldn't duck drinking now — but hell, it was only light wine.

The new ice cubes were almost solid, so we put the other bottle in with a bunch of them. Then we went in front with our cold bottle and it was gone before you could think. But I'd asked her now to tell me about herself. She shrugged those rounded shoulders and grimaced.

"Not much," she said. "The usual thing. And that's what I hate. Starting in a rut and staying in a rut."

A nice rut, though, I thought after she told me. She came from Long Island, around Great Neck. Rich social people. She met this Dixon Grace at some party in New York. He was a partner in a big brokerage concern. That was seven years ago, and they'd bought this place in Jersey five years ago.

"I simply had to get out of that stinking city," she said.

"You mean for artwork? You studied that?"

"Not just painting. Art includes all expressions, and even appreciation of beauty."

"I suppose you've got a beautiful place down at

Bayhaven."

She looked down at her glass. "In a way. Some people think so. My husband does. He thinks it's ravingly beautiful. You know why?" Her eyes looked angry now.

"Why?" I said.

I was amazed at the change in her words and voice. "Because it's so goddamned *big!*" she said. "And because it cost so goddamned much *money!*"

"Oh," I said.

"Oh, *yes*," she said, and waved her hand around. "But take this. It's like a perfect little diamond. Not a great big hunk of a diamond, full of flaws." She stared down then, her hands tight in her lap. She looked as though she were going to cry. I couldn't help it. I went to her. I put my hand under her chin and lifted it. Then I took that soft head and drew it to me. I kissed her. For just an instant her mouth seemed to melt right into mine. Then she drew back sharply. "Oh, no, no, no, *no!*"

All right. I knew something now. I knew enough. I mustn't spoil this. This was enough; a God-given enough. So I looked apologetic, drew away from her, didn't even dare mention the other bottle of champagne.

She was looking at me now almost coolly. And she said briskly, "I really have to go. I really do."

I was scared. I'd frightened her. I'd gone too fast. "I'm sorry," I said. "I didn't mean to do that."

She looked very sad. Then she said, "You meant to, but you shouldn't have, Will."

"No, I shouldn't have. I forgot myself, because you're so very beautiful."

"You really think that? That I'm beautiful?"

"You're the most beautiful woman I've ever seen."

"You *are* sweet, Will. But it's getting late and I *must* go."

She got up then, and I wasn't going to argue. I wasn't going to be a hog. She was looking toward her boat at the dock, and then, without having to glance at the river, I knew the tide. It was the truth and she could go out and look for herself. But I told her. "You can't get downriver in your boat. I'm sorry I didn't think of it before, but time flew so.... From around the bend by Masek's, at this tide, it will be only about a foot of water almost to the bridge — a mile of it. You'd have to have at least four feet for your boat."

"Is that true, Will?" She was looking at me very seriously. "I've never been above the bridge before."

"I couldn't even take you down to Bayhaven in my outboard."

"Even if you could, I couldn't leave my boat here. It might be recognized and cause silly talk. What'll I do now?"

The champagne had affected me more than I'd admit. I was feeling a little lightheaded, but also feeling good: "Let's drink that other bottle and we'll figure it out," I said.

We finished the other bottle, and it must have gone to my head some, anyway, because I said, "Why do you have to go, even when the tide is up? We could have dinner right here."

I hated to see her go. I was just dreading the moment when she'd actually walk to that dock and be off. I might never see her again. Or, if I did, she wouldn't be mellow and as close to me as she now was. And I wanted to see if she'd lie. All women lie, but you like to think they don't with you — you're special.

She lied. She said, "You forget I have a husband. I can't just prance in any time. Especially I can't miss dinner."

It angered me, that lie. It made me suddenly ugly. "You needn't worry about your husband," I said. "He's off with a blondined babe on the good ship *Calypso*. Gone for the night."

For a long time she just sat and stared at me. Well, I'd let the bomb go. I hadn't meant to, and if she hadn't lied I wouldn't have. But the name in that telephone book had been Dixon Grace, Great Oaks, Bayhaven. And on the dock, the tough babe had called the guy who so pompously bought my striper Dixon. Coincidences do happen; that one had, hadn't it?

But I felt sorry, watching her there after I'd spoken. I'd expected angry denial and a generally, high-hat action. But she just sat there, smart enough to know that somehow I knew the answers, not trying to buck it. For then she said softly, "I don't know how you know that, but it's true. But I'd hardly go around telling it. Especially to someone I like and want to like me."

"Me, you mean?" I heard myself saying.

She nodded. "When a man acts like my husband, people can't help but wonder why. There must be some fault in the woman, they think."

That angered me. I said, "But not you. How any man could leave you for even a minute, I can't see. Or if he could have any woman in the world, why he'd look at one of them except you."

At that she smiled sadly. "You're sweet, Will. That was a sweet thing to say."

"I mean it," I said. "I think I'm more of a man than that husband of yours, and I feel that way."

"You are, you are," she said softly. "But there are a lot of things about it you don't understand, Will. It's all mixed up. I am."

I lost myself, I was now so warmed up, pitying her so. I said, "I know how I feel. I'd rather have you than any other woman in the world, if I could have my choice of all of them."

Well, it was out. It was on the line. I sat there shaking, waiting for her to say something. It was a confession, wasn't it? She couldn't brush that off. But she did, in a way. She said, those blue eyes very warm and sad, "That makes me happy, Will. Really it does."

But when I started to move toward her, her eyes changed. She was brisk again. "But I really *must* go. First, though, tell me how you knew. About what you said."

I told her. I told her about the striper and the fifty bucks. I made it as bad as I could, because now I really hated that Dixon Grace. "Just a bunch of lushes," I said, "with whore women. He shoved that money at me as if I was a fish peddler. I don't like that. I could have had a battlefield commission, except the wound put me out. Maybe I didn't go to college, but I could have, on the GI Bill. I still can, when they clear me of this doctor business."

She looked interested then. "What doctor business?"

I told her about the dragged-out, phony business of them checking on me physically every two weeks. "They go through that, keeping veterans on the hook for years, as an excuse to have all these veterans' hospitals operating. Socialized medicine."

"Not necessarily," she said. "I think it's wonderful. A country so thoughtful of its fighting men."

"Was this husband of yours in the war?"

She looked away. "He was deferred because of being in college during the big one. No, he wasn't in the Korean fighting."

I asked her then what, for some reason, I hadn't before. I said, "Have you any children?"

Her voice was almost a whisper. "No, Will. Fortunately, as it turns out."

"What do you mean by that? You'd make a wonderful mother?"

Her eyes were shining with tears, and she shook her head. No more questions. "Would you mix me a drink, Will? Then I must go."

This time she didn't go to the kitchen with me. I took my time out there, because every minute she was in the house I felt happy. Even just knowing she was up front in my Morris chair. From now on, alone in that chair, I could remember that.

I was just pouring the mix in her Tom Collins when there was a rap at the back door. My heart stopped. Could it be Chris, after all I had told her?

I just stood there unmoving, not making a sound. There was a curtained window above the sink, and anyone could look in there. But nobody did. The rap came again, and then the door handle turned. Like a fool, I hadn't locked it from the inside.

The door opened. My heart really stopped now. There stood Rogers, the cop, and with him was Chris.

I got a good smile on and said evenly, "Now what?"

Rogers didn't answer. From behind him, Chris gave me a frightened look. Rogers had closed the door behind him and now stood looking curiously around the kitchen. Then he looked back at me. "Making yourself a drink? So you're one of those lonely ones who don't do it in public."

"Just once in a while," I said. "And I'm always alone."

"Not last night, though," he said, and he smiled a dirty smile.

"Like to join me in one?"

He shook his head. "I'm on duty."

"I thought you hit the beat at night."

He gave me a long look. "Not for a while. Maybe never again. I'm on a special job. Maybe you can help me a little."

"Anything I can do ... What's on your mind, Chris? Forget something here last night?"

Her voice was almost a squeak. "Mr. Rogers saw me at Dillon's and he asked me to come down."

I wanted to keep them out of that front room. I pulled up a couple of chairs. "Sit down and rest your feet," I said. I sat on the little white stool.

Chris sat down, but Rogers didn't. He said casually, "Yeah, they gave me this special job, in line with my old work. Detective work. I just happened to be in the station house when all this data came in. I figured I was the man to dig into it, on account of what happened last night. The Chief agreed."

"What happened last night?"

He gave me that dirty smile. "You should know, Peters. I come down here and find a young girl out on your couch while I'm looking for this Mae Hunt on a complaint. You say you haven't seen her. Miss Humber, here says she didn't see her after a talk they had at Dillon's early in the evening. A Miss Irene Feeny, over at Mrs. Murphy's, says it's definite this Mae told her she packed up to move in with you. Then a call comes in to HQ from the Burton Brothers Laundry, saying a man they sent out on collections yesterday never showed up, and they checked his room, found the bed never was slept in. The man's name was Hunt. So I checked on that, and it turns out he was married to this Mae some years ago and no divorce on record. He's missing with several hundred dollars."

He stopped then and picked up some peanuts from a can I'd opened. He munched on the peanuts as he looked at me. Now it was my turn to talk, he meant.

So I said, "I wouldn't know anything about all that. I told you last night."

"Do you know this Walter Hunt?"

"By sight, is all. I've never had anything to do with him."

"He never made trouble about you and his wife?"

"I never really knew he was married to her until you just told me. She never mentioned him to me."

He popped two more peanuts into his mouth and then leisurely bent over and picked up the empty champagne bottles I'd set under the sink. He held them up, reading the labels, sort of pouting, but casual. "Hmmp!" he said. "Really flying high, Peters. This is imported stuff, runs into big money. I know, because I did hotel work once."

I gave an easy laugh. "If I bought it, yeah. Full bottles. But those were empties I picked up on the beach near Bayhaven. Looked like they might make pretty good net floats."

"Pretty heavy for that," he said, and set them on the drainboard. Then he turned to Chris and said very politely, "Miss Humber, like I told you a while ago, the bartender at Dillon's said you were in a booth with Hunt and his wife last night early."

"That's right," Chris said.

"But you say you don't remember all that was said?"

"That's right, Mr. Rogers."

"You were all drinking, you said?"

Chris was a little more animated at that. "To my sorrow," she said. "And shame. I never do like that. Or buy gin like I did. Or go calling on a man, like I did here."

"Who bought the drinks? This Hunt?"

"He was trying to be polite and pleasant, yes."

Rogers nodded helpfully. "Did he show a lot of money when he did it?"

"I didn't notice," Chris said primly. "I never notice a gentleman's wallet. Or what a check says."

"Was this Mae sober?"

"I don't question other people's condition, Mr. Rogers."

"Did she have a suitcase with her?"

"I couldn't say."

"Was there any quarrel between her and her husband?"

"I really couldn't say. But not while I was there. I left them and went to play the pinball."

"You didn't see whether they left together or separately?"

"No," Chris said, and I could have kissed her.

Rogers turned to me then, and his look scared me, though it was a quiet enough look. He said, "Peters, that barkeep, Jeff, told me you also were in Dillon's last night."

"That's right," I said, mimicking Chris.

"And you bought some drinks for this young girl here."

"That's right," I said. "I like to when I have company at the pinball machine. Give them a little fun, too."

"You gave this young girl so much fun, on top of what that Hunt forced on her, she got intoxicated."

I got sore. "Last night you described her as a bar fly," I said. "When she was out and couldn't hear you."

He winced at that, because now I could see he was playing Chris very politely. But he came out of it quickly. "I mistook her at first for another girl. No offense, Miss Humber."

"Thank you," Chris said formally.

Rogers was staring at me with that quiet but deadly look again. "Did you see either Hunt or his wife in Dillon's, Peters?"

"No," I said.

"Did you see either of them at any time last night?"

"No," I said.

"How did that window of yours get broken?"

"I don't know. I found it that way when I came in last night. Maybe some kids throwing stones from the bank, They do that sometimes."

He nodded, as though to himself. Then he said, almost casually, "You got wounded in Korea, didn't you? In the head?"

"What difference where?" I said.

"It can make a difference in a man's memory," he said, looking hard at me.

"You'd hardly be an expert on Korea or heads," I said.

"Maybe not," he said. "But I've seen some funny things in my business. Car accidents and all."

"Well, my memory is excellent," I said.

"Good," He said. "Maybe then you won't mind if I check on it a little?"

"Go right ahead," I said.

"Tell me in detail what you did yesterday, up to the time I came in here."

Well, I had to. Or get him ugly and suspicious. And I had to tell him the way I'd built it up: downriver until after ten o'clock, selling the clams, taking the basket to Dr. Algee's, leaving the boat at the Bridge Dock, and then going to Dillon's. But when I was through and I saw, or thought I saw, that he was satisfied, that gave me a leg to stand on, and I said indignantly, "You mind telling me now why all this uproar about a woman who beats her room rent and whom you yourself called a common bar fly?"

He watched me steadily while I talked, and for a few seconds afterward, and then he said carefully, "Not at all, Peters. Not at all. This woman didn't only just jump her room rent. She went and got herself murdered. At two-thirty P.M. today, two kids working a killy net down by Morton's old dock dragged her dead body out of the river."

"My God, drowned!" Chris yelped.

"Drowned, hell," Rogers said. "Strangled to death, and her neck broken. The finger marks stood out like a light on her throat." He moved by me, put his hand on the swing door. What he said then was a command, not a question. "You mind if I look through the place once more, Peters?"

Well, here went the ball game. Motive is the first thing they look for. And the best motive in the world for killing a woman is another woman. A more attractive woman. One look at Claire Grace, after my lies, would tell the story.

I couldn't let that beautiful woman, who was getting closer and closer to me, get mixed up in this sordid business. She'd never forgive me — never let me see her again.

So I had to do it. I had to fight. I shoved by Rogers and blocked his way to the swing door. And I raised my voice so Claire Grace could hear. I'd figure out an innocent explanation for her later. Maybe a cop looking for a stolen boat. But I had to warn her, so she could get in that boat of hers and shove off before Rogers saw her.

I said, "I *do* mind! I'm getting good and sore at this insulting questioning. I know nothing about this business and I've tried to make that clear. I've been honest and patient about it. But it's going too far when you want to rummage through my house and invade my privacy as though I were guilty of some crime. Last night you said yourself a search warrant was necessary. Get that, and you can go to it."

His eyes had been hard as nails as I talked, and he'd been fumbling in his pocket. I knew then. I could tell, as his eyes changed, without looking at the paper he stuck under my nose.

"This satisfactory?" he said.

I saw the judge's name and what it said above that. By then he had shoved by me. But that was all right. She was smart. She'd be gone.

But she wasn't gone. She was framed in the open front doorway, her back to us. I knew then, as my heart stopped, that she hadn't caught on, or didn't have quite enough time to make it.

## Chapter Seven

It was like a tableau in that front room. Everyone stood as though fixed in place: the three of us staring at Mrs. Grace, and she staring back at us. Behind her the low sun blazed in, hitting us in the face and making a kind of halo around her bright hair.

For once, even Rogers didn't know what to say. I couldn't have said a word if my life depended on it — as it probably did. Chris sucked in a quick, hard breath.

But Mrs. Grace could talk. She could talk and she could smile. I knew, and only I knew, that she was cool as the morning river. But she didn't act that way. She acted just right. She acted flustered, embarrassed, and apologetic.

"I'm sorry. I didn't mean to intrude. But the door was open, and I thought ... I'm desperately in need of a phone." She waved behind her toward the river. "I hope you don't mind my tying my boat there. I didn't know about the low tide and I got stuck in the mud flats below and had to turn back. I'm afraid my family will be worried if I don't call them, because it looks like quite a delay."

What a woman! I still couldn't talk, but I could look. I put thanks and love in that look, because I knew Rogers wouldn't see it; he was too busy goggling at her. You wouldn't know him, he was so polite now. And he didn't have the slightest reason to ask her name or her business. The very look of her put her automatically out of my class. Not in a thousand years would he dream she'd been my guest for hours before his arrival.

It was very obvious that he fancied himself as a lady's man. Even with a woman like this he tried to make an impression. "There's no phone here," he said, "but this young lady will take you to one." He gave Chris a look then and said softly, "Not Dillon's. Mark's Grocery, on the corner."

"That's awfully nice of you, and I'm very grateful. I just don't want my mother to worry. I've been up the river where it's still deep, visiting friends at Wynnecroft." She smiled then and added, "I'll just have to go back and bore them until the tide is right. When should that be?"

Rogers had to let me answer that, so I did. "About two hours," I said.

She smiled her thanks at me, and added something to it they couldn't get. It was a sort of humorous reminder of the secret between us; an "I'm doing all right, aren't I?" look.

She was doing perfectly, so I nodded.

"Then, if you'll be so kind ...?" she said to Chris.

Chris would have done anything to get out of that house, and she smiled with relief even as her eyes went all over Mrs. Grace, memorizing what she wore and how she looked.

When they were gone, I looked at Rogers. He seemed to have forgotten me. "Well?" I said. "Get on with the ball game."

But he still wasn't ready for me. "God, she was a good-looking woman, wasn't she?"

"I didn't notice," I said. "I've got other things on my mind. What is it you want to look for?"

"Oh," he said. "It's nothing to get sore about, Peters. I've got to complete my report. You and everybody connected with Mae Hunt have to be checked out. Right now I want to look at that broken window."

"I told you about that. It's just an ordinary broken window."

"O.K., if that's the case, we'll just put that down."

I'd meant to repane the window. That morning, when I went down to phone Chris and read the papers, I had the measurements, but forgot to get the glass. When I did remember it later, I thought, what difference? Rogers already knew about it and it was still warm, pleasant weather. I made a big mistake there. I made an awful mistake. Because now Rogers found it was not just an ordinary broken window.

On the bottom, where there were still jagged pieces of glass sticking up, he picked off some tiny pieces of lint I hadn't noticed. He picked them off so fast, and put them in an envelope so fast, that I didn't get a good look at them.

So I didn't know whether they had been torn from my clothes or from Mae Hunt's dress. But then Mrs. Grace and Chris came back from telephoning and Rogers was all politeness again. Mrs. Grace gave me a smile I understood as she thanked me for the use of my dock, nodded to the others, and went down to her boat. We all watched her shove off, turn, and race upriver.

"What a beautiful boat!" Chris said, looking after it.

"One of those Ewing jobs," Rogers said, always knowing it all, having to say it. "Cost more than a good house." He swung on Chris then. "That the dress you wore last night?"

"No," she said. "I don't just have the one dress."

"Describe the dress that Mae Hunt had on. You were with her at Dillon's. So you know. Any woman would."

"Maybe. If I was interested. I wasn't."

"I want to see the dress you wore last night."

"You saw it," she said.

"I saw it in poor light. And I didn't examine it for tears."

"I don't wear torn dresses. Or dirty ones. I took it to the cleaners this morning."

He gave her a thoughtful stare then, and it angered her. She burst out, "What are you trying to do? Frame me into some jam?"

He looked softly at her. "I'm trying to keep you out of one. You're a young, sweet girl who got mixed up in bad company."

"What company?" she said.

He nodded at me. *"There's* a sample."

"I don't know anything he's done. He was a perfect gentleman always with me."

"With you, maybe. Buttering you up. But not with Mae Hunt. See that broken window? He lied about that. No kid broke that with a stone. Or if he did, a woman went in or out of it awful fast later. So fast she left a piece of her dress in the glass."

"Not my dress, I can assure you."

"No. Mae Hunt's dress. And you know how it happened, Miss Humber? I'll tell you. That window was broken from outside. By Mae Hunt. I found the mark of the box she stood on, and marks of high heels in the soft ground outside. She busted in like that while you were passed out by the liquor this man fed you. He couldn't seduce you, so he got you drunk and undressed you to work his will on you. Mae broke in just then, found you unclothed, and went into a violent, jealous rage. This man choked her, broke her neck, and threw the body into the river. He left you as you were, till he cleaned up the evidence of that other woman's being here. Then he'd have waked you, said you'd been out only a few minutes, and he'd have a perfect alibi. He even contrived to put that lie over to you right in front of my face when we brought you to. And you accepted it and repeated it to me. I'm taking this man in on a homicide charge, Miss Humber. But I want to spare you all I can. Do you wish to change your story now? Perhaps remember something that will clear you of any suspicion? You could be charged as an accessory, as it is; and that's the same as though you'd killed her yourself."

I'd taken all I could take. But losing my temper would hurt, not help. So I laughed and shook my head, as though at his hopeless stupidity. "For an FBI schoolboy, you must have missed a lot of classes. Suspicion and proof are miles apart. Even your deductions are way off."

He gave me a wise, smiling look. "Yes? Well, one class taught me plenty, Peters. Police look for four elements in a homicide. Motive, means, opportunity, and consciousness of guilt afterward. You fit perfectly into the first three. Getting rid of a jealous woman you want to supplant with a younger one, those big clam-digging hands of yours, this isolated house where Mae Hunt was always available ..."

I laughed again. "But not consciousness of guilt afterward."

"A man like you wouldn't know what it was like to feel guilty. You probably feel proud of it."

Chris broke in then. "He didn't have any motive — any more than he'd had for months and months. And I undressed myself. You and Mrs. Murphy didn't have any trouble waking me up. You think a fight like you describe wouldn't have waked me? And I was only out a few minutes, because I looked at the radio clock."

He hardened then. He said, "I'm sorry you're mistrusting my interest in you, Miss Humber, and persisting in shielding Peters with that cooked-up story. I must assume you've been in touch with each other today. In that case, much as I dislike to, I'm going to have to lock you up as a material witness."

Her face went white then. Jail. Both of us. And her innocent. But a man like Rogers would railroad us. This was his big chance to reinstate himself from the shame of demotion, and get revenge on me for the ridicule I had brought down on him at the bar that night; ridicule that Chris Humber had witnessed. Whether I was guilty or not wouldn't bother him. He had no other lead, could see no chance of one; and he wouldn't hesitate a minute in framing evidence to support the circumstantial stuff he had worked up.

Nobody would go to bat for me, a friendless clam-digger. And, with Mrs. Murphy's evidence, and maybe some other witnesses he'd dig up at Dillon's, the prosecutor would make a bum of Chris. Attack her character so that her testimony in my favor would be laughed off by the jurors.

I saw all this, and I think Chris did too. Or she never would have done what she then did. It caught me by surprise, and there was nothing I could do before it was too late.

She stiffened up suddenly and color came back into her face. "I can knock all that into a cocked hat," she said confidently. "I didn't tell you before because it was a private matter and none of your business. And I never thought you'd go about accusing innocent people of murder. But if murder's been done, that Walter Hunt did it. He barged in here last night while we were listening to the radio, and he was lusting after Mae. He'd been drinking and said he'd been looking for Mae all over. When we said we hadn't seen her, he left."

Rogers was looking at me now. My mind had been racing. It was out now and I had to make the best of it. The one thing I had to do was agree with anything

Chris said about the time we were together. She was my only witness, my alibi for the time I had to account for since leaving Dr. Algee.

So I nodded agreement with her story. But that didn't satisfy Rogers. He made me repeat it He didn't like it, but there it was.

To any fool, the implication of that testimony was plain. But now Chris, emboldened by Rogers' reaction, made it plainer. She said, "Up at Dillon's Mae confided in me she was washed up with Will, here. She had another guy works over in Freehold. What she must of done is come in here to pick up maybe some stuff she left, maybe broke that window. I wouldn't put it beyond her, gassed up like she gets on that wine. Then she beat it, maybe did the bars with this Freehold guy. So then Walter, he done the rounds, knowing her places, and caught up with her after he left us here. He's missing, ain't he? With a lot of money. So he's on the lam."

There was Rogers' lead, on a platter. Charge Chris and me and have that story taken down by a police recorder and he'd have a red face. Now he had nothing to hold me on; at least, not until he'd picked up Walter Hunt.

He knew that now and he knew I knew it. But I knew something else. It was big stakes for me now, after that story of Chris's. Either I was clear of the whole thing or it was the hot seat. Because now, if they found Walter Hunt's body, with those three slugs in him, there'd be no question who had done it. Not if they could wring from Chris another confession: that Walter had been with me, and alive, when she passed out.

I just had to pray that they'd never find the body of Walter Hunt.

Rogers got in a few cracks before he left with Chris.

About my having come close to obstructing justice, letting the trail cool for Walter Hunt, influencing a young girl to withhold information. He ended by saying, "You're to stick around, Peters. Be available at all times. And keep jogging that convenient memory of yours for more lapses. And I repeat: You're to keep away from this young girl, even by telephone. I can get a legal injunction if you want to split straws on that."

Chris was about to break in then indignantly, but I gave her a warning look and she shut up. I watched them walk up the bank, Rogers solicitously holding Chris by the arm. Then I went back through the house, down to the dock, and watched the last of the sunset.

Mrs. Grace should be coming downriver soon.

It was almost dark when I saw her boat, and when I waved that all was clear, she came in to shore. I wasn't taking any more chances, so I jumped into the boat. "What now?" she said.

"Keep right in the middle, all the way down. Then go for the north shore, after the bridge."

I lit a cigarette and watched her as she steered the boat. My heart was beating like hell. There's an intimacy about being alone in a boat with a woman that no other place can give. You're alone in the world. It's nobody's business what you're doing or where you're going. Especially if you're in the cabin. I wasn't — not yet. But when we anchored in a dark cove on the north shore, I was. And so was she.

She'd put on the riding lights so nothing could hit us. But it was empty over there, anyway. The cabin was tiny, just room for two of us, and it was cozy with the small dome light and little curtains over the windows.

Nothing will bring a man and woman together quicker, or closer, than being conspirators in something, however innocent. A secret. Nobody else knows. Little looks and touches are in order. So I took her hand as her eyes questioned me.

"Do you want to explain, Will?"

"You hear anything? You were there all the time?"

She nodded. "At first I just thought they'd go, that they were just boring neighbors. I couldn't duck out without saying good-by. You'd been so ... so hospitable. So I waited. And then I heard you raise your voice, sort of angry, so I guessed you wanted me to get out. I just wasn't in time. So I did the best I could."

"You played it beautifully."

She squeezed my hand. "Now, *you* do it. Play it all to me. That policeman? And the girl?"

"It really wasn't anything. Just a matter of a stolen boat and a broken window."

She was looking at me strangely, frowning. "But a search warrant, Will? I heard that."

"Big talk. Small-town cop. Let's forget it." My arm went around her. Her hair was touching my face. I was crazy for her. I put my lips against her cheek, and for a moment there she gave way. Then she sat up, away from me. Her eyes had a deep, dark look. "Will," she said, "you're not being frank with me. It was more than that. I didn't really listen until that girl yelled out so that I couldn't help hearing, 'My God, drowned!' Then I heard that policeman say 'murder'. I was afraid to move. I was rooted there. And later, bits of what I heard fell in place as I went upriver, killing time for the tide."

I felt sick now. And I went sullen. Bits, hell! She'd probably listened to it all, as any woman would. To a woman like her, all this was a thrill; a slumming thrill. Later she'd probably regale her pals with the big story. You read all the time about these idle socialites getting kicks out of teasing up truck drivers and cops and cowboys and drummers in bands. Suppose she talked, told about meeting me on the Bayhaven dock in the early afternoon, instead of my having arrived there at ten P.M. as I'd told Rogers? There would go my alibi.

"What is it, Will?" She had come close to me again and was looking up at me with those appealing blue eyes. "Don't you trust me? Once you said you liked me very much."

I forgot everything then. I forgot Rogers and Mae and Walter and Chris Humber. Once my mouth melted into hers, there wasn't anything else in the world. It was like going off into a beautiful death, wanting to die and be in that heaven you could see forever.

No detail of a thing like that could be remembered, except backward, as an unbelievable dream. It wasn't until God knows how long afterward that I could even see. And then it was a blur, a blur of gold hair in my eyes. And then her eyes, staring steadily into mine.

We were on the small, blanketed settee, and she was still close in my arms. Outside I could hear the water lapping at the hull, and the boat swung as a cross-river breeze hit her stem. I put the blanket over her and she shivered closer to me. And then she said:

"*Now,* Will. In a way, we're married now. More than I ever have been. So you can tell me. Tell me everything. I know you're being accused of something, and I want to help."

"It's nothing," I said. "Nothing that you'd want to get mixed up in. But one thing — you never saw me at the Bayhaven dock yesterday. First and only time you ever saw me was asking for that phone at my place."

"Yes, Will. But tell me. I don't care what you did. Not now. Not after what's happened between us. I can't understand that. I've never done or thought of doing such a thing before. It must be fate. Do you still mean what you said to me this afternoon?"

I kissed her. "More than ever. I love you, Claire. If I could have you, I'd be the happiest man on earth. I mean *married* to you. I know, the way it looks, I'm just a clam-digger. But I'm not ignorant or uneducated. I stood way up in high school. I could have made college easily. But they said no, wait until my head was completely healed. But I read a lot; keep abreast of everything."

"Your poor head!" she said, and she kissed the place where the bullet had gone in. "And I love you, Will. I know it now. And I don't think you're an ignorant clamdigger. You work for a living, the hard way, and you're good at it. You could succeed at anything you did."

"But not support a woman like you. Make that kind of money."

"Money hasn't made me happy. But they say misery loves company, Will. I've got mine, so let me hear yours. Sharing them, we'll take some of the curse off."

I sure needed someone to lean on, the spot I was in. With her lying in my arms that way, I felt I could even tell her I'd committed murder. But I hated to let her know what had caused it; the cheap kind of people involved. I'd hate to have her know I could be mixed up with a bag like Mae Hunt, or even Chris Humber. And Walter maybe carried laundry into her house. So I said nothing, tightened my arms around her, and started to draw her close. I had her; the hell with those people.

But she wouldn't let me. She stiffened, pulled away from me. She said, like a hurt kid, "No, Will. Not if you don't love me enough to confide everything in me. All of it."

So I told her what I'd been accused of, but I said the accusation was unjust. I pulled a few punches when it came to describing Mae and our relations. Chris she had seen and talked to, so I couldn't do anything about that. As I talked, she moved back in close to me, and stroked the back of my hand. She acted almost happy; and when I had told her everything I was going to, she said, "I lied a little, Will. I heard everything that was said in the kitchen. So now I know you love me and trust me, because you've told the truth. So far. But not all of it, Will. You didn't tell that policeman the truth — not all of it. Did you, darling?"

"Why should I?" I said. "And be blamed for something I didn't do."

Her head was on my chest and she turned those blue eyes up at me very lovingly and said very lovingly, "For something you *did* do, sweet. When a woman gets as close to a man as I now am with you, she *knows*. Her intuition tells her. Even if you didn't ask me not to mention meeting you on the dock and being at Monte's all afternoon I'd know. But I don't care if you killed a horror of a woman like that. I'd want to kill her myself now if I saw her put a hand on you. Would you want to see a male version of that Mae put his hands on me, darling?"

That wasn't a hypothetical question. Her voice was entirely different and her eyes, watching me, seemed to drag for something deep in me. I knew right then what she meant. And she knew that I knew there existed a "male version" of Mae. I'd seen her husband. The ugly bastard had shoved fifty condescending dollars at me. With an arm around a drunken tart, and a highball glass in the other hand.

But all I could say was: "I couldn't take it if I saw that stinker even put an arm around you."

"But he *can,* darling. And he *will*. As long as he's my husband, he has that right. *Just as long as he's alive.*"

She'd come out with it now. There was no doubt in

this world what she meant. Not to me. I'd already killed two people and she knew it. She'd never tell that, of course. But she was telling me that two murders were as bad as a dozen. As far as the law and punishment were concerned. Maybe so, in theory. But to me, no. I'd done my share, and I'd done it for her. It wouldn't take much intuition for her to understand that. Proof of love should work both ways. So now she could do her share. But I'd have to go slow, putting that idea over, and not make a point of it until it was clearly indicated. Until then I'd let her think I was not only ready, but eager to do it, but wasn't going to be too crude in mentioning it.

So I gave her a deep look that needed only a few words to go with it. Those words were: "Maybe he won't live much longer."

"Ah!" she said, and she dug her head into my chest. "Oh, Will, how I do love you!"

If ever a woman tried to prove it, she did after that....

Later, she dropped me off at a quiet, unused dock below the bridge and I walked home. Nothing definite had been settled about her husband. I had let her think he was in the bag, but that my movements were being watched too closely now by Rogers. We'd have to wait until this Mae thing died down.

She saw the virtue in that. But she wasn't taking any chances of my cooling off because of the necessary delay. So, for over an hour before I left her, she poured it on. She let the dam open wide on her hate for Dixon Grace. She said he was a drunk, a chaser, had squandered the money she'd given him to invest, and that now he was taking dope, which was the last straw. Whatever he took, it made him into a beast. He'd force himself on her when he was under its influence, and treat her shamefully. To prove it, she showed me scars and nasty-looking black-and-blue spots.

When I asked her why she hadn't divorced him, she said he wouldn't let her go, and that she couldn't get the legal goods on him. In public he always put on a loving act. It had been her money he'd used for his race-track betting, his women, and his dope. He was canny as hell with his own. But if he died she'd get it back, and more, because he'd have to leave the property and his own hoarded money to her. And his insurance.

I got in my point then, not pushing it, but intending to work on it later. Why hadn't she killed him herself? I didn't say it outright, just hinted at it.

"I've thought of it," she told me. "But do you remember the rules for the prime suspect that your policeman recited to you? Motive, means, opportunity? Well, I'm the perfect qualifier where Dixon is concerned. When a man's murdered, police dig up information nobody ever suspected before. People will talk who wouldn't peep in a divorce action. The first one they check is the one who would profit most from the murder. And anyone previously connected with him would be questioned and checked. But not you. Will. As far as the police are concerned, you're never even heard of the man. Those are the cases that are never solved."

I let it go at that. I could always change my mind.

I was thinking that as I walked by Dillon's. It was rocking, as usual. I wondered if Chris was in there. I didn't want to see her, stir Rogers up. I was keeping out of Dillon's from now on.

I went down the bank to my dark house. There was a light on in Masek's shack and his radio was going. I wondered if Rogers had questioned him, and I was tempted to ask him.

But I decided against it. Let sleeping dogs lie. And sea gulls and cats, too. I had other things on my mind.

Something she had said gave me an idea. A perfect idea. I knew how she could kill her husband without the slightest suspicion. But I'd let that lie for a while so as to get the credit for good intentions.

## Chapter Eight

All that next week I worked hard. I wanted to get my mind off the mess, and besides, if Rogers was keeping tabs on me, I wanted it to look as if I considered the matter closed as far as I was concerned. They didn't even have an inquest over Mae. It turned out, from what I read in the paper, that the doctors didn't agree there'd been foul play. Nothing lurid came out. They found enough water in her lungs so that she could have drowned. And a body banging down that snag and rock-infested river could easily have a broken neck.

Another thing I found out: smart-aleck Rogers hadn't matched that cloth scrap with the clothes found on Mae. Because if he had, he'd have been at me again. I knew why. Mae had torn her dress breaking in that window, but she'd had her suitcase along, and she simply changed her dress and put the torn one back in the suitcase. Well, they hadn't found the suitcase, and never would; so I was all right.

I sent a nice wreath to the funeral: "From an Old Friend." But I didn't go.

Claire Grace and I had decided that, when I thought it was right, I'd phone her. She told me the time of day, and who to say I was. We'd already arranged where we'd meet.

Those days I read every word in the local papers and listened every minute I was at home to the radio; never missed the news. Because if they found Walter, things would really blaze. It would be too much of a coincidence. And Walter with three bullets in him. No snags or rocks could do that.

Two things about that week I didn't like. I've always said that women never know where to stop; they won't let well enough alone. A man can be having an affair with a woman and no one would ever guess. But the woman can't help giving the show away.

Even a smart woman like Claire Grace. I might or might not have seen her red cruiser on the river before I met her; I couldn't say. But now I saw it. She went by three times that week that I saw, but I never even glanced at her. Just gave her my back and bent to my rake, trying to tell her to cut it out. She could queer things that way. The talk among the other clammers was already making me sore. The remarks they made about her bare legs and all. One of them, a guy named Andy Love, went too far, and I nearly hit him with my rake.

Then Chris Humber. *She* couldn't let well enough alone. Not two days after I saw her with Rogers at the place, she sent me a letter. The gist of it was that I should phone her. She could get a car and we could drive far from Rogers, for a few hours, anyway. She also said she loved me.

I had to phone her to cool her off. But maybe her phone was tapped, so I had to be cagey and try to tip her. You can't; not with a woman like that. "But all that's over," she said. "A poor woman drownded, is all. Who could blame her if she commits suicide with that Walter breathing down her neck? I got to see you, honey. I love you. Like I even put down in black and white on paper."

"The ink was green," I said, trying to make it light. "I'm working awful hard to catch up on the days I missed. I'm tired out at night. You be just like you were with you-know-who-I-mean, and I'll call you the end of the week."

She was a little edgy then. "Be like I was? Try and keep that party like *he* was!"

I jumped at that. "What do you mean?"

"Now he's trying to date me, social. Not just low dives like some men try. He invited me to the Volunteer Firemen's Ball. And he asked me to dinner at the Shadowland Inn."

That meant his intentions were honorable, in her book. But I didn't like it. That babe loved liquor; and like all of them, she talked more than she should when she drank.

I tried to warn her and I think I put it over, because she said, "So I make you jealous, I'm happy. Don't worry. I'll be faithful. Won't even look at another man. Maybe we can go to Asbury? No one knows us there."

"O.K.," I said. "I'll call you. Just stick to what you already said and add nothing if you're questioned."

She kissed into the phone as I hung up.

I met Claire Grace at the end of the week; did it just as we'd planned. She same in that red boat into the north cove right after dark. The tide was as I'd known it would be, and she came right in so I could wade out and chin myself aboard. I'd pulled my light boat up out of sight and we went out and anchored in the warm dark.

In the cabin I took her in my arms, and once again I forgot the whole mess. Now there were just the two of us in that dark, cozy cabin.

But she said no. "We've got to talk, Will, and I have to be back."

"He's out, isn't he? You said he always went on weekends with that bunch of morons. They make a night of it, don't they?"

"Yes. Before. But I'm not sure now, Will. He's found

out something. He beat me last night."

"Found out what?"

"I don't know how much, for sure. But he knew we were in Monte's. He taunted me about it."

"About *me?*"

"I don't know."

"What did he say? His exact words?" I didn't like this.

She seemed to think, and then she said, "He said, 'You're not kidding me, you faking, cold-blooded little, bitch. Maybe if I want some action, I should take you to Monte's Inn and do a little jukeboxing. That seems to heat you up.'"

"You ever dance there before?"

"No."

"That sly bartender told him, maybe?"

"Carl? I don't think so. He was steward of the Club before he opened that place. We all go there. Carl sees some funny things. But talking would ruin his business. Someone who knew me must have come in while we were dancing and we didn't notice."

"The hell with him," I said. "Come here."

"No, Will, we've got to get this settled *now*. I've thought of a plan. It's simple and safe. Look."

She turned on the light then and pointed to it, where it was lying on some waxed paper on the settee. It wasn't big, but it was a beauty. It would run to about twelve pounds, and it gleamed silver and green on that white paper: a striped bass.

"I trolled to the lower bridge, and then coming up here, just for the looks of things. I never dreamed I'd catch anything. But it was fate, Will. It fits right in. Because he didn't go out today. After that scene last night, he went into one of those dope debauches. He even flaunted the needle in my face. 'One thing that loves me, anyway,' he kept yelling. 'One hot thing I've got that nobody can dance away from me.'"

"You mean he's home now?"

"Yes. Hung over badly, and with one of those fits of remorse. He even pretended he didn't know what he said or did last night. That and the fish make it perfect — don't you see?"

"No," I said. I hadn't seen anything perfect for a long time, except her.

She was shaking with it now, and her words poured out. "We go right downriver now, both of us. But you stay in the cabin. Our place is right on the beach. I'll buoy this boat in deep water about a hundred yards out, then pick up the outboard dinghy I left at the buoy, and go in. Tonight I'll show him this striper and tell him they're jumping all over out there. One thing he can't resist is sure-thing trolling. Part of his ugliness lately has been because his fishing luck has been so bad. With him, fishing is as much of an addiction as booze or drugs. Once it was his only one, and it's still there, deep in him. Sort of a last relic of decency. He makes a fetish of it — a last gasp at manhood."

She was breathless, clinging to me now, so I left the edge off what I said. I said, "So when you flaunt that striper, he'll want to go right out and show you how it's really done. And you'll be the forgiving wife, and sporting mate, and lead him to me, who'll be waiting to knock him off when he comes aboard."

She shuddered against me. "No, Will. I couldn't do that. I couldn't be a Judas. And you forget, I've got to be above suspicion. My part will be done when I handle him just right so that nothing could keep him from a run up and down the river to pick up at least two bigger fish. Then your part comes, darling. But be very quiet. You hide right here, see. And do it before he gets any lights on. And then you bring the boat back here, pick up your own boat from where it is now, and just let him and my boat drift. There's no way in the world anyone can possibly connect you with it."

I didn't say anything. I knew what I was going to say — but not now. This was too soon. So I bent down and felt for her mouth. She let me kiss her, but it was different. Her mind wasn't on it. I tried again, and then I lifted her. But she stiffened and struggled against me.

"No, Will."

I felt a sudden ugliness. Just go and knock off her husband, but let's don't bother about any love. The hell with that. "What's the matter with you?" I said.

She was away from me, her hands out. I could see the gleam of her eyes, even in the dark. "Will," she said, "please understand. What happened the last time was fate. I was swept away. I was so emotionally aroused that I lost all sense of shame. But I've had time to think it over. Then, it seemed that we could never be anything, really, to each other. That the obstacles were too great. But now I see with a greater vision. This isn't just some transient infatuation. This is something that can be made very beautiful, and sacred. By marriage, I mean. Surely, knowing how I feel, you can wait? Later, you'll be glad that I wasn't the sort to go sneaking around, making love in cars and boats, breaking my marriage vows."

"We couldn't be married for a long time. If you're so hipped on convention, you know that."

"We'd be married in the sight of God," she said. "It wouldn't be a sin then."

This was almost as pious as Chris at her best, and I thought, They sure as hell are, all of them, sisters under the skin. She wasn't fooling me. She wasn't hot for anything now but getting rid of that husband, and fast.

"All right," I said, "you've told me your plan. If it wasn't for one thing, I'd do it like a shot, and you know it. But that one thing could hang both of us and I don't want you hanged."

"No. It's foolproof, darling."

"Not after that unknown told him he saw us dancing to the jukebox. He may have told others. Your husband may have told one of those morons he fishes with. You say you never danced in there before, but you did with me. That was worth noticing by somebody."

"But nobody would know who you were, darling!"

"Maybe not. I'm thinking of you. Because one thing they *would* know is that someone murdered him on this boat. Why? A man wouldn't do that for robbery. A man fishing doesn't carry much money. There'd have to be another motive. And you'd be the best-looking motive in sight. Those cops would track back on every move you've made lately. Your picture would be in the papers. That cop Rogers would see it and so would Chris, and recognize you as the poor stranded woman in my house. And Masek, whom you asked where I lived, would see it."

"My God!" she said.

"Yes. If he dies now, or later, *by violence,* a woman who looks like you is going to have her picture blazing out of every newspaper in sight. He's got to die another way. And I know just what way. I got to thinking what you told me about him using dope, and I remembered a newspaper story I read. You probably read it, too. A man said to be an addict died under mysterious circumstances. Circumstantial evidence pointed to foul play. But the autopsy doctors said he died of natural causes. That decision was contested, and top toxicologists admitted that if he'd taken a shot of unadulterated heroin, instead of the usual diluted shots they use, he would have died of that. It's a sure thing. But if he's an addict, it doesn't show up in the blood, and so they attribute death to natural causes. Usually pneumonia or heart attack."

She had been listening so hard that she barely breathed. But she didn't say anything, so I went on: "You said he bragged about the stuff, so he doesn't hide it?"

"No," she said in a whisper.

"Did he ever try to get you to take any?"

"Yes," she said.

"Then you can show an interest. Pretend to flirt with the idea. Find out which is the undiluted stuff. Switch it on him in place of the regular stuff he uses."

I stopped talking then. For years, it seemed, there was no sound in that cabin but the little slaps of waves against the hull, and some far-off sea gulls complaining as usual. I wondered for some strange reason if Masek's Wilbur was on the wing. He usually took off at dusk. But then I began to wonder why she didn't say anything and I asked her, and she said — really piously — "Why, Will, that would be *murder!*"

"That's what I thought. So?"

"But I couldn't do a thing like that! A *wife,* murder her *husband?*"

"Plenty of them have. Some, even, for love — to hear them tell it. But hate's even a better reason."

Her hand tightened on mine. She said softly, "Of course you're right, Will. Logically, I mean. And I would do it; I'd do it for you. But I've lied to you, Will. I thought I had to, so that you would hate him the way *I* do. Because lots of men drink to excess and hit their wives, and other men don't think they deserve to be killed for it. But drugs are different. All normal men hate that. They can see how unbearable it would be to a woman, and the addict is better off dead."

"What are you trying to tell me?"

"I lied about his taking dope, Will. It's just liquor and meanness. So I couldn't do what you suggested."

Here was a mess. She knew how I felt and how to handle it. She had to backtrack a little now, give a little. Because if she had that intuition she bragged of, she must know that now, sore as I was, I wouldn't carry out *any* plan tonight.

I thought that then. I had reason to think it. Because she came into my arms and her mouth was eager and asking. No stiffness now. This was asking for forgiveness, and for an implied promise from me that we would start from scratch, make a new plan. One that *I'd* carry through.

When I left her, a couple of hours later, my promise was more than implied. She had shown me a love that no one else had got from her, and that I hadn't even dreamed of. Addict or not, Dixon Grace was not long for this world. I told her to think up a new plan and I'd do it within a week. But I'd think of a better one — for *her* to do....

The last thing she said as I held her in my arms before going over the side was: "Oh, darling, just think! A week from now we'll belong to each other forever and forever!"

I tingled with those words all the long way home.

But I tingled in another way when I got there. There was a small inboard boat at my dock that I let Parks, the gas-station man, tie up there. He'd put an old convertible top from an automobile over the front, and it was dark in there. When I tied up I saw the blur of movement in it and then heard Chris Humber's voice. "Will! Come in here!"

I jumped in and glared at her. "What are you doing here, after what I told you?"

"I had to, Will. But nobody saw me. I came down by the dump and walked along through the weeds. I've been waiting over an hour."

"That wouldn't throw a crumb like Rogers off."

"We're safe from him. He's off duty tonight. He's in Trenton on some business. I know, because he wanted me to drive up with him, but I said I had to visit my sister in South Amboy. Aren't you going to kiss me, honey?"

Well, she was here, she'd been seeing Rogers, and maybe there were some things I could find out. So I kissed her and she clung to me as though she were drowning. "Let's go into the house," she said, shivering against me.

That I didn't want. This was business; for me, anyway. So I steadied her down, asked her what, if anything, she had learned from Rogers. I heard more than I expected. Maybe the damned fool *had* fallen for her, because she told me he'd questioned Masek and taken her with him at the time. When she told me what had happened at Masek's, I began to get the drift. This Rogers fancied himself as a lady's man, but also as a detective genius. His vanity made him less a detective than a lady's man, because no good cop would take a girl along when he questioned a supposed witness, just to impress her. But Rogers had done it. And he'd made a mistake by it, if her story was right. She said:

"He was awful mean to that old man. You know, sarcastic and all. Sneering at the way he had them animals talk. I thought it was sort of cute. But Rogers was real mean."

"Can you remember the exact words?"

"They weren't nice in front of a lady, and I told him so later. Imagine! He said to that poor old man, 'Listen, you drunken old sonofabitch, don't give me that nut stuff! Talk to me direct, and look at me when you talk!'"

"What did Masek say?"

"The cat said it. She said, 'What disgusting language in the presence of ladies!' I really had to laugh at that, hon. Mr. Masek's really a good ventriloquist."

"What was said about me?"

"Rogers wanted to know if the old man had been home that night. The sea gull said, 'You can't prove it by me. I'd flown down to pick up my unemployment insurance check.'"

"What did the cat and dog say?"

"They were all there. They saw and heard nothing. You can't argue with animals, hon. So then Rogers said like I told you. And he cursed out about the privy the old man has there. Said he was going to have the Sanitary Board raise hell with him. But he needn't report it if Masek would co-operate."

"Meaning accuse me of something?"

"I gathered that, hon. But why are we bothering about all that water over the dam? Whyn't we just go into the house and forget the whole thing? I'll tidy things up while you get a nice bottle of gin."

Not in my house. Not me. But when I started to make that clear to her, she threw the bombshell at me. At first I didn't even guess what she was getting at, she was so coy and clinging. But she hardened when she decided I couldn't or wouldn't understand. I went cold all over when she came out with it. In the dark there I stared at her and wished with all that was in me that I'd thrown her into the river that night. But I had to keep cool; I had to beat this. So I said humoringly, "That's impossible. In the first place, I didn't lay a hand on you that night, and in the second, it's too short a time for you to know whether anything like that's happened."

She said softly, but with ice in the words, "In the first place, I never, never personally took my clothes off that night, asleep or not. It's against my nature, and I know myself. In the second place, a woman can tell those things, faster even than any doctor. But to make sure, I went to a doctor, because I knew something had happened to me that night. They have tests now that can be pretty sure this early. He said yes."

I just stared at her in the gloom. And then she took my hand and sort of whined. "But aren't you happy, hon? Just you and me now? No Mae, or nothing. Just us and the little one. But we got to be married right off."

I was thinking of that bastard Walter. If she was right, he'd really had the last laugh. He'd been faster than I could have guessed. But that wasn't helping now. I'd done all that could be done with him. Now I had Chris to worry about.

I thought awfully fast then. I could tell her Walter did it, but she'd buck that, whether she believed me or not. Walter wasn't here, and I was. Walter was a widower, all right, but not the sort she'd want to proclaim as the father of her child. I was the sort; she'd made that plain. And there was another thing: If I admitted I'd left him alone with her, why had I done it? If I said I'd gone to Dillon's for a new bottle of gin, Jeff would say I'd done no such thing. I was in a hell of a spot.

But when you're in a fix like that, the thing to do is play them, as you do a big fish. Don't fight them. Pretend to give. Make the best of it. Time is always on your side. Who knows what can happen in a few days, or even hours?

So I did that. I had to. I let her make it easy for me when she said, "All is, hon, I just want to know you love me. I can forgive how it happened. You were drinking, something you never do, and I got you drinking. So I'm responsible for the way you acted. Only thing, I wisht I could of been conscious, missing out on our first love like that. But you ain't been drinking now and I ain't, so you tell me and I'll know. Then you can go up and get us a nice bottle of gin."

I had to do it. I had to play it right. But believe me, in that dark house, with Chris and the gin I got, I suffered terrible pangs of conscience when I thought of beautiful Claire Grace, who really *did* love me. And when I practically had to shove her out, just before dawn, for the first time in my life I sat down in the Morris chair and cried. Maybe it was because my head hurt so terribly....

## Chapter Nine

The next week started all right. First thing, I strolled over to Masek's with a little something for the animals and some cold beer for the old man. I guessed he knew why I was doing it, but that didn't take the virtue from it, because I also knew by now that Masek, for some reason, liked me. True, I always waved to him when I went by in the boat, and never missed tossing some clams. The cat liked them almost as much as the sea gull, and finally the dog got to gobbling them. Masek tossed them down raw, like peanuts, with his beer.

Of course, I didn't bring up the subject of Rogers' questioning, but the cat did. She said a nasty policeman had been over there and she had stuck her tongue out at him and run him off.

What did he want? I asked.

Just being nosy. So nosy he even objected to their rustic little bathroom. That didn't take too much nosiness, I noticed.

"That can be remedied," I said, "by running a pipe to my septic tank, which is right close. Put in some old secondhand plumbing fixtures and everything will be jake."

"Wouldn't give the bastard the satisfaction," the sea gull said. He actually dropped a big load on his stump as he said it.

That was all I wanted to know, so I took off downriver and worked hard all day. I was making good money, and I wanted to keep it up. Money is man's best friend, I've always thought. I'd told Chris that. I was stalling her on that basis. But she didn't guess I was stalling. She thought I was just being very fair with her.

I had put it this way: Let's wait until she was sure. If she was in that shape, then we'd get married at once. But I wanted her to go to my doctor a little later; a man I trusted, and who knew his business. The one she'd gone to I'd heard was a quack, I had told her. So if he was wrong, then we could do it right. No hurry. I wanted to build up my bank account. It was the best clam season in years, and by winter I'd have us a stake that would buy a car, put in TV, help her out on a handsome trousseau, and pay for a honeymoon in Miami.

That appealed to her. A big, fancy wedding, and a trip out of a state she'd never left. She could laugh at Rogers and the bums at Dillon's. She even put it that way, piously happy. She said, "Not only that, hon, but with our new-found happiness, you'll be spurred on to bigger things. No need a man like you breaking your back with them clam rakes. You got brains, so make them other bums work for you. Leave them dig them, and you wholesale them. They all know you and would rather sell them to you than them gyp dealers. You can buy a swell truck and even finance boats. And look, hon; never, never do we go into that crumby

Dillon's again. And we don't drink no quart of gin a day — jest a small pint. Oh, I'm so happy, hon!"

I was crawling. But I played it all right.

That was the day before I saw it in the paper. I'd been watching those papers and listening to the radio daily for possible news of Walter. I read every word so as to be sure. But this was right on the front page, and you couldn't miss it. Dixon Grace dies at his home in Bayhaven. Death attributed to a heart attack. His wife, the former Claire Belew, prostrated with grief and under a doctor's care. The well-known sportsman and investment broker had been ill recently, but had refused to seek medical attention, his wife reported.

It went on like that, giving his and her background in a laudatory way. But I wasn't interested in that. Just the big fact held me spellbound. Maybe she'd done it and maybe she hadn't; but if she hadn't it was the world's greatest coincidence. And I'd be pretty dumb if I couldn't figure it, after that last talk we'd had on her boat.

She'd lied to me, she said, about his taking dope. She'd lied, all right — about his *not* taking it. But I didn't blame her for it. I admired her. Only *she* would know now that her husband was a dope addict. You could be sure that, after she switched that heroin on him and she knew she had him, every vestige of evidence that he used the stuff would be gone from that big estate in Bayhaven.

The more I thought of it, the happier I became. What she'd done was clear as a bell to me, though I would never let her know that. When I'd last seen her, I'd promised to kill the man, and she'd believed me. I'd lied, but she'd never know that, either. She'd known right then that she was going to do it, if what I'd told her about a full shot of heroin was true. What she'd wanted to be sure of was that I loved her enough to risk my life for her. Once she was sure of that, she was ready and willing to do her bit. But she didn't want me to know that. Not after that "beautiful and sacred" talk. If a man thought the woman he loved had murdered her previous husband, it would always be there in the back of his mind every time they had even a lover's spat. I didn't blame her for that. I admired her.

It was far, far better this way.

I wanted to phone her right away. But I knew better. The little squib in the paper about her being under a doctor's care, prostrated with grief, was smart. That would keep the nosies away from her and tip me to take it easy.

Oh, I felt wonderful that day. It was in the morning paper, which I always read before taking off. So then I went downriver, and luck was still with me. I got into a bed I thought was long dug out, and loaded the boat. I gotten bushels of cherrystones, took in over fifty bucks for the day.

She couldn't phone, but she could write a note. Maybe a love letter. She wouldn't need to sign it, would she? It was too soon yet. But I watched my mailbox on the bank. Tomorrow I'd get one.

I could wait, but it was hard waiting. I kept seeing her face all the time. Working that damned rake back and forth, hour after hour, I kept seeing her face.

I couldn't stand Chris now. I'd been patient, played along with her, not knowing what was going to happen, keeping her easy, but I couldn't keep it up. Now I knew what was going to happen. I knew soon I'd sell my boats and my house, and then, with what I had in the bank, I'd have enough to take me far from here, set me up well, and dress me just as well as Dixon Grace had ever dressed.

I knew how to do it. I'd go to the best clothing place

in New York and be honest with them. Tell them I'd come into some money and wanted to dress the part. In a place, say, like Miami. I'd always wanted to go there. There I'd be far from Chris and from Rogers and from where they'd buried poor Mae. And I'd be far from anything they might ever find of Walter. But I was sure by now that Walter was far out to sea and never would be found.

I'd have my honeymoon in Miami, all right. But not with that ungrammatical Chris Humber. I'd come to more than dislike her, but I didn't dare run her away when I'd find her lurking in that boat nights as I came back from downriver. I couldn't make love to her, not now. So I made a virtue of that: I pulled a Claire Grace in reverse. Marriage was too beautiful and sacred to anticipate in a sacrilegious way. It actually made a hit with Chris; too big a hit, because then she did something that made me hate her. Really hate her.

Somehow, in the house she must have picked up Dr. Algee's note to me, and read it. It was just a reminder that I was overdue for my checkup. So that told her who my doctor was, and she decided to play it cute, and maybe please me. What she really was doing was taking me at my word and hurrying that sacred marriage up.

I discovered what had happened when I reported to the doctor's that night. He didn't mention it until he'd talked a while and let me talk a while, telling what I'd been doing and all. Then he came at me in a half-joking way.

"That's not all you've been doing, Will. Come on, 'fess up, now."

"All that's important."

He frowned then. "A young lady came to see me today. A Miss Christine Humber, Will."

It was like a bullet in the heart. But I said carelessly,

"Oh?"

"You know her, of course?" He was smiling again. "She said you sent her."

"Sure," I said. "Sure, I know her. But I didn't send her."

"She said she was pregnant by you, Will. I questioned her and examined her, and she may be in that condition."

"Not by me, though."

"She said you were going to get married."

"You believe that, Doctor?"

"She seemed like a nice, healthy girl. And to think a lot of you, Will. The only thing ..." He began poking at his dead pipe, not looking at me. "I'd rather ... at this time, well ... it's not my business to determine paternity. If another man is to blame, I'd like it better, Will. Because, you see, that head of yours is ... well, not just what I'd want in a young married man. Not that it's anything transmittable, but marriage brings a great change in a man's manner of living. No matter how great the love, there are petty annoyances almost daily; annoyances that the sort of free, open-air life you've always lived will leave you utterly unprepared for."

He suffered a little, telling me that. I suffered more. Because now it was on the line. Always before he had belittled that hole in my head. Nothing to it that time wouldn't cure. But time had passed. Three years had passed, and here he was, trying to tell me that marriage would drive me nuts.

Christine would, hole or no hole. But what about Claire? I suddenly got ugly there, and I shot a lot of stuff at him I was sorry for afterward. I told him *I* knew how I felt, it was *my* head, and already I'd had plenty of annoyances in my life that hadn't driven me nuts.

I didn't realize, at the time, that I was actually proving his theory on the spot by my wild raving. But he let me go on, watching me, and I finally caught on to that and shut up. I tried to be very cool, and said I was sorry, but being falsely charged with paternity would make any man mad.

But he had more to say.

"Another thing ... I almost forgot. A few days back, a policeman called on me, Will. He was asking about you. He mentioned the clams you brought me, so I assumed you must have talked to him first. What was that about, Will?"

This was getting worse. That sonofabitch Rogers! So he'd checked my alibi story. I said carelessly, "Stolen clams and a stolen boat. He questioned all of us on the river. Just routine."

"Oh, glad to hear that, because it upset me a little. I thought maybe you'd had a fight. Do you ever have ugly spells, get sore at people, want to hit them, Will?"

I laughed. "I'm as easygoing as they come, Doctor. What did this cop want to know especially?"

"What time you brought the clams. And if, and why, I was treating you."

"Around ten at night," I said. "Yes. And you're not treating me."

"That's right," he said, and I felt a little better.

When I got up to go, he said, "I'm sorry this paternity thing has come up. But the legal end is something you'll have to handle yourself, Will. Of course, if you were intimate with the girl, you have certain responsibilities."

"I wasn't. I swear it, Doctor."

"If that's so, then simply make it plain to her."

"I'll certainly do that, Doctor," I said. And I meant it.

He shook my hand warmly as I left, and said, "Now, always remember this, Will. I'm not just your doctor,

I'm your friend. Don't hesitate to come to me any time with your troubles. An ounce of prevention is worth a pound of cure, you know. And good advice can be excellent prevention."

He meant well, but I wondered what he'd think if he knew all the prevention he'd missed so far.

When I left him I was terribly tempted to phone Claire Grace. I just wanted to hear her voice. On my way to my boat, I passed Monte's Inn. That's where I'd first held her hand, first called her Claire. Where I'd first held her in my arms as we danced to the jukebox.

What did it was the music I could hear faintly in there. It was the same piece we'd both liked and had danced to several times. So I went in. I was dressed all right, even for the sport crowd sitting on those red leather bar stools, and dancing; I had on a sport coat that had cost me plenty, and a nice pair of gabardine slacks. But one look at those people, the type Claire had meant when she had said, "We all go there. Carl sees some funny things," made me realize he'd never seen anything as funny as a guy ordering a Coke in there. So I had a beer.

Maybe I'd have gone out after that, even noticing the telephone booth as I did; but a fat blonde on the stool next to me said to the man on her other side, "Wasn't that simply terrible about poor Dixon?"

"Awful. And just the day before it happened, I was talking to him, kidding there on the dock. Looked the picture of health."

"Poor Claire! They say she's distracted. Can't eat or sleep. I wonder what she's going to do."

"Don't worry about poor Claire," another woman chimed in. "She'll have plenty. And *her* looks are more than the picture of health."

I found myself drinking beer now only as a chaser. I

had a double shot at my elbow. I drank that. And then another, hoping to hear more; but they got off on another subject, and that telephone booth looked bigger and bigger to me, until I couldn't stand it any longer.

I went in, shut the door carefully, and called her. When a servant answered, I used the name she had told me to use before. The servant said, "Mrs. Grace isn't receiving any calls at this time." But just then Claire's voice came on. She must have been listening from an extension.

My heart leaped. I loved that voice. I knew, of course, that I couldn't say what I wanted to, and neither could she. All I could do was express my sympathy for her in her great sorrow. That I did, and she thanked me in a soft voice. But under those sad tones, I was sure there was love to burn. So I added, "If there's anything, anything at all, that I can do, please let me know right away, won't you?"

"That's awfully kind and thoughtful of you," she said.

I got bolder then. "Just drop me a note. You know how to address it."

"Yes," she said. "That's very sweet and kind of you. I'll do it. Good night, and thank you again."

I went out of that bar almost singing. Her soft sad words were still warming my heart. Maybe she'd write that note as soon as she hung up the phone. It could be in my mailbox tomorrow morning. It would be. The mail didn't come till ten, so I'd just let the early clamming go, but I could put the morning hours to good use. Several real-estate firms had contacted me in the past about selling the place. One had a buyer waiting. And I knew they had sounded out Masek. His place and mine would make enough space for a string of small tourist courts, now that the new toll road from New York had been completed.

I knew just where I could sell my boats and outboard. I figured I could get maybe six thousand for the house and land, and five hundred for the rest. Add that to the five thousand I had collecting interest in the bank, and I could put up a pretty good, show until Claire and I were married.

One thing I knew: I wouldn't ever live off her. But it would be all right to let her finance me. We'd keep the red cruiser; that had too many lovable memories to let go. Besides, I'd need it to get started. That dumb Chris hadn't been too far off when she said I had brains enough to quit the muscle work. I couldn't ever work indoors, of course. Dr. Algee was right about that, but for the wrong reason. It had nothing to do with my head. Even with no hole in my head, I'd go nuts working at a desk.

I knew what I'd do. I'd been dreaming about it since the last time I saw her. In Florida, I'd build up a fleet of boats like her red one. We'd rent them out with trained crews for sports fishermen with money. Maybe we'd buy one of those Florida keys, and put up a palatial fishing camp there; the ultimate in luxury. With her looks and social position and contacts, it couldn't miss. Me she could explain easily enough. She'd gone down there to recuperate, met me, and married me. Why not? The way I'd look then would make that first husband of hers look like a busboy. She could explain the early remarriage by saying she was just swept off her feet. People of her social type are used to quick changes in marriage. I could even take her and the boat down through the Inland Waterway ...

I never felt happier in my life than when I jumped out of bed the next morning. I had a swell breakfast: grapefruit juice, good thick lean bacon, three poached eggs, and some hot corn muffins. I'd figured what to do about Chris: nothing. Never let on I knew she'd gone to Dr. Algee's. Let her tell it if she wanted to. But it wouldn't do her any good, because I'd be gone where nobody but one would know, in a very few days.

I made the deal with the real-estate office, after they'd looked the place over, dickered a bit, and said it would take a few days for a title search and some other red tape. They made it $6,500. I did nothing about the boats and the outboard because I had to work up to the last minute, so as not to arouse Chris's suspicions. Rogers I hadn't seen for some time, and hoped never to see again.

But I saw him. I saw him worse than I'd ever seen him before. And this time he really had something to make me sweat.

They'd found Walter Hunt's body.

I read it in the paper after I left the real-estate office, on my way to the mailbox. I'd tingled in spite of Walter as I pulled out that tin cover. But my heart dropped when I saw the box was empty.

And when I got back to the house, empty-handed, empty-hearted, there was Rogers, waiting for me.

## Chapter Ten

This time Rogers didn't have Chris with him, but he wasn't alone. He had a state trooper with him. One look at that big fellow, and I knew this was going to be different. Those Jersey state cops are the best in the business. They don't say much, and they don't butt in on local police. But if they're needed, or if there's a question of jurisdiction, they're right in your lap. And once they get their teeth into a job, they never let go.

I let them into the house and Rogers showed the

state cop around, talking very professionally as he pointed out everything, reviewed the case up to that moment, and at last asked him if there was anything more he'd like to ask or to see. From what he'd said, I gathered that they'd already questioned Masek again.

Then Rogers said, "Peters, the state police are interested because there's a question of jurisdiction. You can clear that up, here and now. I've worked on this case since it started. And it started right in this shack. But Walter Hunt's body was found out of the city. So it will simplify things and be best for you, too, if you make your confession right here in the presence of Trooper Kane. If that satisfies him, then we can go down to city headquarters and take it in writing, and the trooper here can get back to his own work."

One thing was clear: Rogers wasn't going to let anyone steal his thunder. As far as he could, he was going to make this a one-man job. A job that would spread his name all over the papers and make him again a sergeant of detectives.

Not if I could help it. I looked at the state trooper. "When you're ready to take me to your barracks, I'm ready to go, Officer," I said.

For the first time he looked embarrassed. He couldn't let his fellow cop down. It wouldn't be ethical. And a confession can be made anywhere. More often than not, it's easier to extract at the murder scene than in a cold and fearsome police headquarters.

So the trooper said quietly, "If you are prepared to make a confession or have anything pertinent to say, it might at least clear up the jurisdictional angle. But I must inform you that anything you say may be used against you, Peters."

"I have nothing to say; at least, not to this flatfoot here. He fancies himself a detective, in spite of the fact that they demoted him to a beat. He's trying to build himself up at my expense. He's made himself into a local bully boy and he doesn't care who the hell he frames so long as he profits by it."

What I was saying was dangerous. I wasn't helping myself. Because I was putting this decent state cop in an embarrassing position with a fellow officer. But I couldn't help it. Watching that smug, nasty-eyed Rogers, sitting there putting on his act, infuriated me. It made my head suddenly seem to flame. I saw the trooper's jaw harden and his eyes turn cold on me, but I kept it up.

"Another thing," I said. "A young lady I go with — he's continually annoying her. He keeps pestering her to go drinking and dancing with him. He never dares come near me when he's off duty and out of uniform because he knows what I'd do to him."

The state cop spoke then. His voice was very quiet, but his words were cold as ice. "What *would* you do to him?" he said.

I knew I'd gone too far then. I'd alienated whatever sympathy I could have expected from him, and I'd done worse: I'd indicated a homicidal tendency. Or that's the way Rogers would put it.

With a great effort I calmed myself. "What you'd do in my place," I said.

The trooper stood up then. He said, "You'd better come down to the barracks with me, Peters."

If he'd said, "I'm taking you to the barracks, Peters," Rogers would have been in a spot. But this was within the city limits and state cops never force any issue there. Not unless it's been agreed on. Rogers didn't make that request. It was exactly what he didn't want. Now he said, putting on a nice act, and smiling:

"Take it easy, Peters. I know how you feel. I don't blame you for being upset. Or even misunderstanding my motives. But I have a duty to perform, and I have to do it the best way I know how. Naturally I had to play up to Miss Humber a little, hoping for a slip. I don't need that now. I have everything tied up. If Officer Kane will bear with me a few minutes. I'll give it all to you." He looked at the trooper hopefully and said, "I don't give you the full picture, Kane. Perhaps there's something in what Peters says. I have been trying to build myself up professionally, a bit. I hope you can understand that, and bear with me. And that Peters will see that there's no point to gain by complicating this with separate authorities."

This was better for me, now that I was calmer, and had done a little thinking. I'd find something out, and I didn't have to say a word. But I wouldn't stress that point now. So I said, "I don't want to complicate it. I just don't want to be blamed for something I didn't do. If you think you have proof, give me a chance to deny it. Right now, I don't even know what I'm being charged with."

Rogers said, "You're being charged with the homicide by strangulation of one Mae Hunt and with the homicide by shooting of one Walter Hunt, on the night of August twelfth, current year, on these present premises."

He had whipped some typewritten sheets from his coat and had been pompously reading. Now he looked over the sheets at Kane and the trooper nodded for him to go on. He went on:

"Motive: Disposition of Mae Hunt, because tired of her and to make way for a younger and more attractive woman. Disposition of Walter Hunt, because he either suspected or knew of fate of wife, and would have borne such witness.

"Means: Throttling by hand in case of Mae Hunt, shooting by thirty-two-caliber revolver in case of Walter Hunt. Weapon not yet found. Bodies of both thrown in river as means of disposal. Two bullets extracted from head of Walter Hunt."

The trooper interrupted then. He said mildly, "I understood the woman was pronounced dead by drowning?"

"That was moot," Rogers said. "They'll exhume her body now in the light of this new development and make a more careful autopsy."

I spoke up then. Too much silence might be bad. "I don't see what this has to do with me," I said. "Any man can throttle and shoot a pistol."

"That's right," Rogers said smugly. "But we're interested here in the man who had the best opportunity to do it." He lifted the paper again and read, "Opportunity," then cleared his throat. The trooper lit a cigarette, after surprisingly handing me one, and then he sat down. I couldn't tell whether he was bored or interested.

"Opportunity," Rogers repeated. "The victim, Mae Hunt, was a habitual visitor at the domicile of the accused, William Peters. It was general knowledge that they co-habited, this constituting adultery, as the victim, Mae Hunt, was at that time married. Evidence proffered by Irene Feeny, Three-twenty-six Brook Street, is to effect that on August twelfth Mae Hunt declared she was moving in with William Peters permanently as his common-law wife."

He went on then, reading away, going over the same old ground. I was beginning to feel better. I'd been absolved of the killing of Mae, and, as I'd said, anyone could have shot Walter. But then, as he read on, I remembered. That "opportunity" was the bad thing. Chris and I had admitted Walter had been here that night; and, as Rogers got to that part of his spiel, I noted the sudden gleam in the trooper's eyes. Circumstantial evidence indicated that Mae had broken into this house; actual evidence showed that Walter *had* been in the house, looking for her.

But I still could have fought that. I could have if Rogers hadn't suddenly sprung his hole card on me. Up to now he'd been playing cat-and-mouse with me, and the big painstaking detective with Trooper Kane. Because when it came out I realized Kane was a late-comer and didn't know all the evidence. But now he knew it.

I touched it off myself. In a pause in Rogers' reading, I said to him, "That's old stuff. It's only your interpretation of it that tends to implicate me."

"That's right," he said, and he laid down the papers. "There's more at the end, though, that isn't old stuff. It just backs up the key piece. You want that now, Peters? It can save time."

I felt suddenly dry all the way down my throat. Was it about Claire? Had he tied her in with it? I had to know.

I heard myself saying, as though I were someone else, far, far away, "Sure, let's have it now."

It was a letter from the grave. It was a letter from Mae Hunt to her husband, Walter Hunt, that had been found on his body with his wallet. It read:

Walter, you dirty louse:
I've taken all I'm going to from you. Your talk in Dillon's about being a new man and let bygones be bygones left me cold, but I was too much of a lady to let that out before those moronic bystanders. So when you left I came back and wrote this so as to leave no lingering doubt in your mind, knowing you would be back whimpering and telling your business to all and sundry, and after more booze. So I told Jeff the bartender to give this note to you. Once and for all, NO. I'm going to Will's right now

and this time stay there with a man who knows more about loving a woman than you ever dreamed of. You come whining around Will's house and you'll get a .32 in your dumb head. Because Will wouldn't soil his hands on you, but use your own gun I took from you and couldn't hock. He's been saving it for just that purpose. So Stay Away.

Your never loving wife,

Mae PETERS (from now on)

Well, there it was. There was their motive. They didn't have to charge me with killing Mae. The job on Walter would send me to the chair. Mae's last wino bragging had done it. I'd never mentioned Walter to her, but try and prove it. They knew he'd been here, and they guessed what happened to him. And why. What more did they need to know?

"Where's the gun, Peters?"

"That's all a lie," I said.

My mind was working again. They had damning stuff, but it was still only the letter of a wino. They didn't have a witness. But I had a witness. If Chris stuck by me, swore she was conscious all the time that Walter had been in the house, had seen no gun, and that there'd been no quarrel between us, what could they do?

"What did you do with the gun, Peters?"

"I've never had a gun. But Mae said *she* had a gun. You just read it. A woman can shoot a gun as well as a man, you know."

"Not with a broken neck, though. Or break her own neck afterward. And a man with three slugs in his head couldn't do it."

The trooper said then, "You admitted, I understand, that Walter Hunt was here that night?"

I nodded. "But I have a witness that was present all

the time. She saw him come and go. In good health. In fact, he was even bragging about his health."

The trooper glanced at Rogers then, and Rogers gave him a fancy police look. Then he said, "If you've no objection, Kane, I'll take this man in right now. Anything more you want to ask him?"

There wasn't much Kane could do. It was now obviously Rogers' case. So he shook his head. "We'd like to be kept informed, though. Will you do that?"

"Sure will," Rogers said happily.

Before I knew it, he had a pair of handcuffs on me and said, "Let's go, Peters. You can make that confession downtown."

As Rogers led me toward the riverbank, we passed Old Man Masek's place. As we went by, clear as a bell came the words "If it ain't that sonofabitch Rogers!"

The state trooper stared at Wilbur incredulously. Rogers rose to the bait angrily. "I'll get you for that, Masek! Insulting an officer while performing his duty. And for something else more serious, which you'll hear about soon enough."

"Nuts!" the sea gull yelled again.

I couldn't help it; cuffs or no cuffs, I burst out laughing. The state cop gave me a sour look, and I said, "You just heard a talking sea gull. Anyone ask me, I'll testify to it under oath."

"All we're asking you, Peters, is get up that bank and in that car!" Rogers raged.

As we went by the empty mailbox my spirits dropped lower. If I'd only got that letter this morning, had read her loving words, I could take this. Because I'd have memorized those words. They'd have lain warm in my heart all through what was to come. No cops' words, harsh and ugly and threatening, could have bothered me while I had them.

But there had been no letter.

When they got me to police headquarters they took me to a room, and they really worked me over. It wasn't just Rogers now. A D.A. was there, two real detectives, a police surgeon, and, of course, Rogers — big and important now.

He had put it over, too. I could tell that by the way even the Chief of Police deferred to him. And they listened deferentially to what he had to say. I didn't listen deferentially, but I listened. And when they at last locked me in a cell for the night, I knew it was even worse than I'd thought. Because new stuff had come out. And I knew that after this Rogers would never have to walk a beat again.

He must have spent every waking hour since the beginning in deadly, persistent quest. He'd failed with Dr. Algee and my phony alibi of selling the clams at the dock, but pointed out that I could have done the killings later, either before I met Chris or while she was passed out. The D.A. interrupted politely then. "But the girl says she was conscious all the time Hunt was there and saw him leave. And yet our best chance for getting a conviction is to charge him with the murder of Walter Hunt."

"Hunt could have come back while Miss Humber was unconscious," Rogers said. "It only takes a moment to shoot a man."

"But the sound of a shot would have brought her to."

Rogers looked wise. "Maybe not, in the awful condition he had that girl in."

"And maybe she's lying to protect him," one of the detectives said. There was a man who knew his job. But Rogers wasn't letting him catch him out. He gave that wise look and said, "Maybe. I've given, and *am* giving, that angle a lot of thought."

That's when my heart stopped again. If they broke

down Chris's story, I was sunk. But I was sure she was loyal. As far as she knew, I loved her and was going to marry her. In a way, I'd had a break. If I'd run out on her, and they'd found Walter, and brought me back from Miami on a fugitive warrant, she'd have turned on me. A woman scorned. They really ruin you.

There were some other things that were bad, though. Rogers had checked the pawnshops, as a result of Mae's reference to trying to hock the gun, in her note to Walter. He found the place where they had turned her down, so that meant she did have a gun that I would have had access to.

And they'd brought Masek in. I saw a uniformed man go by the open door with him before they shut it. Maybe they wanted me to see him. They'd sweat him later in another room. I wondered what he'd do without the animals to answer for him. And I wondered if he'd break and say that he had heard shots that night.

When at last they let up on me and lead me to a cell, I saw Chris. That was staged, too, I suppose. A cop had brought her in, and Rogers joined her in the hall. He was smiling and very polite. But she wasn't looking at him; she was looking at me. Her eyes fastened on those big handcuffs, and she started to cry and called my name. I asked if I could talk to her a moment, but they said no. And one of the detectives said, "It was talking to her too much that got you in this jam. Remember the story of the cat and the streetcar?"

The hell with all of them. Because, as I passed Chris, the look she gave me had all the love in the world in it. It wasn't as good as a note from Claire, but it was something to take to that hot, stinking cell. It was hope.

## Chapter Eleven

They wouldn't let anyone see me but my lawyer. Dr. Algee sent him the minute he heard of my arrest. It was in all the papers, of course, played up big. The jailer let me see a couple of them, but just the headlines. "CLAM-DIGGER ACCUSED OF DOUBLE KILLING." And there were subheads like "Glam-digger clams up."

The lawyer's name was Braden, and from the polite treatment he received, I guessed he was an important one. He'd evidently been carefully coached by Dr. Algee as to my background and temperament, because he didn't go right at me, ask me to lay it all on the line. He said, "I've had a long talk with the District Attorney, Peters. He was very frank with me. They've got a strong case. Circumstantial, of course, but that's implicit in most murder accusations. In a first-degree case, a man doesn't kill in front of witnesses. And first degree is what they are going to work for. You know what conviction for that means?"

"The chair, yes. But my defense isn't circumstantial. I have a witness, Miss Humber, who was with me from the time I gave Dr. Algee the clams until the police came and took her away."

"It would have been possible for you to do it *after* that."

"Only a fool would kill after that police attention. They were looking for Mae Hunt when they came to my place."

He nodded at that. Then he said, watching me carefully, "I've gone over this with Dr. Algee, of course. This girl you mention as a witness is the same one who came to him for a prenatal examination, I understand?"

"Yes," I said, and I felt a little cold in that hot cell.

"You denied paternity, didn't you?"

That was a trick question. That was something Chris must never know. That could turn her against me, sink me. So I said, "I was ashamed to admit it. I was a little sore at her at the time, because I told her just to be examined, like any other patient. Not to mention me."

"I see," he said. Then he gave me a hard look. "But you never denied it to her, did you?"

"Oh, no," I said virtuously.

"Was marriage mentioned between you?"

"Yes," I said. "Just as soon as we were sure. Can you see her, Mr. Braden, reassure her? But not mention what I said to Dr. Algee?"

"Yes," he said. "She'll be our witness, of course. Unless ..." He looked away from me then and began fiddling with his glasses. I waited. I knew something was coming now, something bad.

"Unless what?" I said.

"Unless we don't go to trial," he said quietly.

"You mean I might not be indicted?"

"You're certain to be indicted. Unless something else happens first."

"What, for instance?"

He let me have it then. I should have known. He said, "Unless you are declared mentally irresponsible. Now, Peters! Wait a minute. Listen to me."

I had jumped to my feet. He couldn't miss the ugliness in me. He let me get it out for a spell, and then, when I'd quieted a bit, he said, "You say you'd rather go to the chair as a murderer than be declared a nut. That's stupid, Peters. In your case there's no stigma connected with it. Quite the opposite. You were wounded in the service of your country. You received a Purple Heart and a Silver Star. If anyone is to blame, it's the Red rat that put that slug in you. And another thing: your case is curable, Dr. Algee tells me. Just a matter of time. Sure, they'd put you away for a time. But suppose you go to trial and they *don't* give you the chair? Suppose they give you life? That *could* make you nuts, Peters, an outdoor type like you."

I was still shaking. I said, "They'll never give *me* life. Before I'd take that I'd give them a confession that would ensure the chair. And as for 'putting me away for a time' in some nut house, that would be worse than convicting me of murder, in *any* degree. And furthermore, I wasn't just over in Korea to enjoy the scenery, and I wasn't pecking a typewriter miles behind the lines. I was right in the front lines for eighteen months. I was fighting. And I led a platoon of fighting men. I didn't quit then and I'm not going to quit now. Let them throw all the circumstances at me they want, but they'll never get me to admit one damned thing. You can go back and tell your friend the D.A. that. And Dr. Algee."

"The D.A.'s no friend of mine. I hate the sonofabitch. I'd like nothing better than fighting him."

"All right. And you can tell Dr. Algee that if he testifies I'm nuts — "

He got mad then. "For Christ's sake, Peters, Dr. Algee's the best friend you've got in the world. Do you know what my fee is for a major case like this? That *he's* offered to pay?"

"I don't know and I don't give a damn. But I've got enough to pay for the priceless information and help you've already given me. Get me a pen and checkbook and I'll prove it. I don't take charity, either."

He got up then and laughed. He slapped me on the back. I glared at him. "You think I'm nuts?" I said.

He laughed again. "Hell, no! Peters, do you know what a grand old man of the law said to me when I first started practice? Admit nothing and deny everything. You want me to work with you on that basis? Because I'm a fighter, too, once I'm thrown into it."

He held out his hand and I took it. I even smiled. I even liked him.

"On that basis, yes," I said.

"All right, then," he said. "Sit down there and tell me anything and everything that will give me a chance to win this fight."

I told him anything and everything as Chris and I would tell it if we took the stand. But not once did I ever hint that I disliked Walter and Mae Hunt, much less that I had murdered them.

When he left I felt fine. I had a witness who could save me, and a lawyer who knew not only how to use that witness, but how to knock hell out of Rogers' evidence. What I didn't know, at the time, was that Rogers had witnesses, too. And that he wasn't resting on his laurels. No, Rogers was still busy as a bird dog; and his business paid off.

He had found time, too, to work on me. Twice before my lawyer first came, he and the D.A. had tried to wheedle a confession out of me. I told them they were wasting their time, and I could see that they believed it. I also saw that the D.A. was worried. He didn't do the bragging Rogers did, or make the hints that more evidence would soon be forthcoming. He admitted he had barely enough, but it would convince a jury. On the other hand, why keep the lurid business going, to the detriment of the good name of the city, and at great expense to the taxpayers? How about settling for a second-degree rap?

I told both of them just what the sea gull had yelled at Rogers, and there wasn't a damned thing they could do about it. But the D.A. said, ugly now, "All right,

Peters. You've asked, for it, and you'll get the works. We're holding Masek as a material witness without bail, and it's only a question of time before he breaks and talks. He knows plenty."

He turned out to be more right than he knew. The blow fell the day after I'd talked to the lawyer. They let me have it, all of it, because they were certain it would shock me into a quick confession. Rogers must have pleaded to be allowed to bring me that news, because he came in all alone. It wasn't Masek that had broken and talked; it was Chris.

Chris had ratted on me. He showed me her statement, all neatly typed, and let me read it. In it she admitted that her first story had been false in several particulars. I had invited her to my house; she hadn't invited herself. At Dillon's, earlier, Mae had a suitcase, and had told her she was going to move in with me. She had passed out on my couch while Walter Hunt and I were still talking. She had not seen him leave, as she had previously stated. We had quarreled.

Rogers was jubilant. "Peters, you found Mae Hunt in your house before you talked to Miss Humber in Dillon's. She broke that window to get in, you got sore and killed her, then chucked her body in the river. Then you went to Dillon's and invited Miss Humber to your house as a cover-up. You note she says Walter Hunt came down there, raging, thinking she was his wife, and you had a fight. But you knew he suspected you, so you soaped him up, probably doped that drink of Miss Humber's to put her out, shot Hunt, and threw his body in the river. Later you told her he had left amicably. Then you did a rotten thing, Peters. You put on a big love act with that young girl. She fell for it. Of course she was willing to lie for you, especially as she thought you were innocent and wanted to marry her. But she knows what a louse you are now, Peters."

He stopped then, glaring at me.

I think at first it was the shock of Chris's turning on me that scared me, rather than what she had admitted. In a few seconds, though, I shook myself together. After all, I didn't love Chris. Even before this, I'd almost come to hate her. I loved Claire Grace. If *she* had done this to me, I might have quit there and then, let them do what they pleased.

So now I glared back at Rogers. "You make me laugh," I said. "A girl you called a bar fly in front of two witnesses changes her story. She says I told her to lie. Can she prove it? And even if I did, that doesn't prove I killed anyone. What do you expect when you give a young girl like that the third degree? Bring her here to face me and let's see what she says."

I'd walked right into the little door Rogers had opened for me. I could see that by the way his eyes lit up greedily. But he kept his voice quiet as he held up a letter. He said, "This proved far more of an incentive than any third degree, Peters."

It was Rogers' big moment as he shoved it close so I could read it. I had never seen her handwriting, but I knew it. It was like her: round and smooth and beautiful. And the words were loving and beautiful — as a cyanide cocktail. Because those words were going to send me right to the electric chair.

Rogers had been busy, all right; so busy that he had watched my mail, picked from my box the first letter I ever got from Claire Grace, known exactly what to do with it. He, too, knew that a woman scorned could ruin you. One look at that letter and Chris Humber would have signed anything that would hurt me.

Because Claire had laid it on thick. She said she loved me, loved me, loved me. That she couldn't wait until we were married. But that we had to be careful, not see each other until "certain things" blew over. I mustn't phone again until she dropped me a note telling me when and how to do it. Then, if only for a few glorious hours, we could be in each other's arms again. Probably in New York.

She hadn't signed it, of course. But that didn't make any difference. Who she was wasn't a must for Rogers and the D.A. Here was their motive, and maybe now Chris was remembering that affectionate choking scene, her own throat in my hands, just before Walter came.

But they did know it was mailed in Bayhaven, because Rogers showed me the postmark on the envelope. And he said, "We'll find that hot baby, too, Peters. I'm working on that now. And from the writing, the choice of words, and the mail address, it's obvious she's pretty well up in the social scale. She won't like being dragged into this. But she doesn't have to be. If you'll talk now, make a full confession, we'll just leave her a Miss — or Mrs.—X."

His dirty little eyes were really greedy now. This could be the biggest day of his life. He was pulling so hard for my answer that he was shaking.

He got my answer. He got the same answer the sea gull had given him. But they let me send for my lawyer, and he came that night.

"She's their witness now," Braden said grimly. "Peters, if you'd been properly frank with me, this might have been foreseen and stopped."

"You can't stop the U.S. mail."

"Do you want to tell me about this new angle of the case? This other woman?"

"No," I said.

"Rogers will dig her up. He'll make a bad, bloody show of this."

That scared me. "How can he?"

"If she's a Bayhaven woman. Whether you like it or

not, he's a damned good detective. He's proved that. He's got the paper she wrote on. There's a possibility he can trace it to the sales outlet. And there's her handwriting. If she has voted anywhere in the area, he can check the voting registers. She has to sign that with her name and address."

I went really cold on that. If Rogers thought of that, he'd find her — if she voted. I was almost ready to give up. If Rogers ever traced Claire, and discovered — as he would — that her husband had just died in the prime of life, his agile brain would put more than two and two together. He wouldn't stop until he had her in jail, too.

Braden was eying me in that careful way again. He said, "I had quite a talk with the Humber girl after I was here before. This Bayhaven note hadn't come out then, of course. You must have really given her a big snow job, Peters. I see now, of course, that what you told Dr. Algee about her was the truth. You had no intention of marrying her. But she was deadly serious about it. Not just because of her condition, but because she really loves you, Peters."

"She sure showed it in a funny way," I said bitterly.

"She showed it the way women always show it. The transition from love to hate in a woman can be instant."

"So I noticed," I said.

He had his glasses on and was giving me that creepy look over them, but his voice was soft and quiet as he said, "And vice versa, Peters."

"What do you mean?"

"The transition from hate to love can be just as fast."

"They wouldn't let me talk to her. How could I change her?"

"I can talk to her. But I've got to have something to say, Peters. More than you'd say if it were left to you."

"What would I say?"

"The usual. That it was all a mistake. The dame meant nothing to you. Just an odd job you'd got mixed up with before you fell for Chris."

"What's wrong with that?"

"It's not subject to proof. It's talk, not action."

"What proof or action is there?"

"That's up to you, Peters. But I can tell you the law. In a criminal case, a man's wife cannot be compelled to testify against him."

I sat very still there, watching his cool eyes. He took off his glasses and rubbed them with a handkerchief. Then he said, "But she can take the stand in his defense. She can say, if they admit it in evidence — which I'd fight — that the statement they got from her was obtained by duress, or on a promise to let you off easy. Lots of things."

He stopped and watched me carefully again. I didn't say a word. I wanted him to go on, and he did. He said, "She could tell such a sympathetic story so that a jury would, at least, disagree. She's a pretty little thing with a nice voice, and she could dress quietly and lay off that gin for a few days. Maybe."

I didn't say a word.

He went on: "As for the letter-writer from Bayhaven, your action in marrying the Humber girl would knock that out as a motive. It wouldn't fool the D.A. or Rogers, maybe, but they'd gain nothing and lose lots by dragging a woman into the case just to smear her. No jury would like that — not unless she was vitally relevant. And she wouldn't be, once your romance with the Humber girl was publicized. The newspapers would eat that up. How she stuck by you when all hands were against you. Insisted on marrying you, to hell with the charges against you. And, if they railroaded you to prison, by God, she'd wait if it was a lifetime."

My laugh must have been pretty bitter, but he seemed to expect that, and he lit a cigarette leisurely, not looking at me.

"You forget a few things," I said. "First, I'm not out on bail, but in a stinking cell. They don't let you get married in jail. Second, I'd lose, however the trial came out. If I won, I'd lose. I'd have that gin-drinking babe on my neck for life. Unless I murdered her the way they say I did the others. Even Dr. Algee warned me against such a marriage. He said a man like me couldn't take it."

He smiled then. "He meant, take it for long."

"I could never shake her off."

He thumbed his glasses, rubbed them again. "You mentioned having quite a sum of money in the bank. I'm not asking for any of that. Not if you take my advice. Love wears off with women the same as with men, Peters. Love for men. But never for money. An amicable parting in a reasonable time after the trial should prove simple. And, as for not being allowed to marry in jail, you forget that girl's condition. If she weren't pregnant by you, maybe not. But if you so state, I can arrange for the marriage to take place. And the sooner the better, naturally."

I looked at him. He was tapping the ash from his cigarette into the coffee-tin cover they gave me for an ash tray. He was doing it delicately and carefully, as though it were the most important job in the world. At last he looked up at me. "Well?"

"I'll think about it," I said.

"I'd think fast," he said. "Before she goes to some quack doctor and maybe adds another death to the picture."

I was cold as ice in that hot cell when he left me, smiling.

## Chapter Twelve

Chris and I were married in a small upstairs room in the jail. I didn't ask Rogers to be my best man, but he was there, and he looked far worse than any disappointed suitor. He was ugly as hell, but he never said a word. I wondered why Kane, the state cop, was there; he was, but kept in the background.

The D.A. was there, and my lawyer, and Dr. Algee. I couldn't look Dr. Algee in the eye, but he shook hands with me and said a few encouraging words before he left. The clergyman who married us was connected with the state prison system, so it was all in the day's work to him. I had asked that Masek be allowed to attend as best man. I still had a little sense of humor left. But Rogers had heard me ask the D.A., and he had raged at that. "That wise-guy sonofabitch is going to talk yet! We may have lost one witness, because of the tricks of a shyster lawyer, but we'll break Masek down yet. A man who lives and acts like him you can be sure has got a record. Maybe not locally, but we've sent his prints to the FBI, and the good news ought to be in any day. And when it comes, Peters, you'd better really squeeze them. I've done a lot of checking on Masek's habits. He doesn't spend all his time making Charlie McCarthys of animals. He's a night owl, and I've had the doctor check his hearing. He heard those shots, all right, and maybe a lot more. And he saw plenty, too."

I agreed with all that — mentally. But not that Masek would talk.

Chris had been almost sober at the wedding. They didn't let me talk to her alone either before or after it. But she held my hand like grim death while it was going on, and the looks she gave me begged my forgiveness and promised all her love from then on.

It was kind of pathetic, the one thing she did ask for. But they wouldn't let her, wife or not. They said she couldn't live in my house because it was sealed and would have to stay that way until after the trial.

Braden protested that, but got nowhere. He also made a plea to the D.A. to drop the case now for lack of evidence. He got nowhere on that. Dr. Algee had brought a big bunch of handsome flowers, picked on his own place, he told Chris, and she cried as he gave them to her and patted her hand.

The last I saw of her, she was looking tearfully at me over that bunch of flowers.

No reporters had been allowed at the wedding, but they were thick in the hall downstairs. They were waiting for Chris, and all I hoped was that she hadn't brought some gin in her purse and taken a belt or two in the toilet before she met them.

But she probably had. The wedding story was all over the late papers. The jailer showed me them. In one picture she looked cockeyed as hell; little hat askew, tears running down her cheeks, and those flowers jammed up against her breast. They quoted her as saying: "Will's the kindest, sweetest man ever lived. He wouldn't kill a sparrow."

I felt like killing *her*. I wondered how Claire would take it when she saw those papers. She'd understand. Or would she? There hadn't been any publicity about Chris's statement, so Braden had told me. "That would make their faces look too red," he assured me.

I'd told Claire about Chris's being with me that night, and it had been in the papers; but she knew Chris meant nothing to me, and that *she* meant everything. She'd understand, all right.

But the grand jury didn't. They met a few days later

and they indicted me fast as hell after the D.A. laid it on thick to them. He said he was going to ask for first degree, expected strong additional evidence, and hinted that it would sew the thing up tight.

Braden was worried. He pumped me about Masek, begged me to try to remember every little thing I could about him. "I've done a little checking myself," he said. "Nobody in the neighborhood knows anything about him. They seem to think he was just a harmless eccentric, living alone there with his three animals. But what worries me is that he receives no Social Security check, has no visible means of support."

"What did they do with the animals?"

"Rogers jumped right into that, of course. I've heard that Masek begged to have them brought to his cell. The cat and the dog. The sea gull, of course, has probably taken off for greener waters. Rogers realized they're the man's very life. He's on a hunger strike, has been all along. But he can't see the animals until he talks; then he can go home."

"Has Rogers got them?"

"The bastard sent them to the pound. He's cruel, too. I learned all this from your new wife, Peters. She wanted to take them, keep them in your house until they let Masek out. But no soap."

I told him what Rogers had said about checking Masek for a record. His eyes looked like pin points then. His voice broke like a young boy's. I thought he'd hit me. "For Christ's sake, why didn't you tell me that before? The very instant you saw me?"

"Why?"

"*Why!* Record, hell! If he's done his time, O.K. Even if it was twenty years for second-degree murder. But if he *hasn't?* If he's been wanted for years? A fugitive? Now they'll grab him because of his prints. Oh, my God, Peters, don't you see? He'd *have* to make a deal.

Add that to wanting his animals — his very life — and you spell Guilty with a great big capital G. You, brother!"

I realized then that he thought I was guilty himself. I felt cold as ice. I said, trying to still the beating in my head, "If he could do it, *I* can."

He was thinking, thinking hard. He didn't answer.

"I can escape. I can hide out like Masek in some far place. See these hands? Look." I took the heavy washbasin and squeezed it flat before his face. Then I pointed to the bars in the little window of the cell. "Those are old and rusty. I can do the same with them. They're not going to burn me because of some crazy fugitive's love of animals."

"Wait a minute, Peters. Take it easy. It's unethical for me to listen to talk like that. I'm an officer of the court. Now listen: It's a gamble, but I'm going to take it. I'm going to offer my legal services to Masek. I'm going to get his damned dog and cat out of that pound and treat them like royalty. And I'm going to shake heaven and earth to get Masek out on a writ. What's the most you could put up for his bond?"

"Eleven thousand, if I sell my house."

"You won't have to sell it. Ten thousand should do it. Is it worth it to you if Masek should jump that bail?"

"Yes," I said.

I had new hope then; more than before, because until that talk with Braden, I hadn't realized how much their case depended on Masek. They were certain all the killing had been done on my premises. And, close as Masek was, night owl that he was, and never leaving his place, he must have heard it, probably seen it. His very attitude, his stubbornness in not even talking to them, had convinced them he had guilty knowledge. Even if his record proved to be clean, they still had the cat and dog to hold over his head. That was the chink in his armor, ana they were going to pry it bigger and bigger until he talked. He owed me nothing, but his very *life* was those talking animals. I comforted myself with the thought that he'd never have talked to Rogers as he'd done if he were a wanted man. I didn't know then how loneliness and hate can destroy a man's self-control.

I had hope until late that night, when Rogers came into my cell. He threw it at me the way he might news of a big win at the races. He gloated over it. They had refused to issue a writ of habeas corpus for Masek. There wasn't a chance of his getting out until he told what he knew.

"I'll believe that when my lawyer tells me," I said.

"I wouldn't be surprised if Braden withdrew. Probably ashamed to show his face around here. In view of what just came in, Peters. Hot from the FBI in Washington."

I knew then. I hardly listened as he recited it. Braden's worst fears had been realized. Masek, under another name, was wanted in Michigan on a murder charge ten years old.

"Of course he'd cover for a fellow killer, Peters. That is, as long as it didn't hurt him. But extradition to Michigan will hurt hell out of him. The only animals he'd have to talk to there would be cons like himself. He won't choose that alternative, Peters. Not if he talks for the state. He's had a clean record here for ten years. Add those two elements, and it doesn't make for extradition."

"Has he talked?" I said. "I've never heard him talk yet."

"This time he'll do it straight. And that's the thing for you to do, right now, Peters. An honest confession, added to that wound in your head, would make things easier for you."

Once again I said what the sea gull had said to him. He cursed me as he went out.

There was only one way left. There was no word from Braden when I needed him most. Masek would talk, and I couldn't blame him. No word from Claire since that damning letter, and I couldn't blame her, either. She was keeping abreast of things by reading the papers, of course. She knew I had a good lawyer and, up to now, had a good chance of beating the charge, now that I was married to Chris.

I looked up at the barred window. It was an old jail, and I was in the last cell in the block. There was a dimly lighted passage between the cells, but no lights were allowed in them this late. The cell across from me was empty, and it was quiet the rest of the way down, everyone asleep. The best thing of all was that I was on the ground floor. Outside was a tree-shaded yard.

I couldn't squeeze those bars with my hands, of course. Nobody could. But I could do wonders with the iron pipe frame of my bunk. All I needed was the end piece of pipe. If it was strong enough, if it held up, I could prize those rusty bars apart like river reeds.

It was tough getting that pipe. It took all I had to bend it back and forth till it broke at both ends. And it bent as I prized at those bars. I had to be quiet and careful, but at last I made it. It was a tight squeeze. For a while there I was jammed and thought I wouldn't make it. Then I thought of Rogers' finding me like that, laughing up at me. It cut me, it bruised me, but I tore loose. And when I dropped to the ground, it was dark and very quiet outside.

I had thought out just what I was going to do. I'd already withdrawn all the money in my savings account the morning I'd made the real-estate deal in preparation for my run-out to Florida. I'd stashed it in my house. So I had to go there, and fast. Because, once I was missed, that would be the first place they'd look for me. Later they'd know I'd been there, but that wouldn't make any difference.

They'd boarded up the broken window, but I got in there, after sneaking through back streets and coming to the house along the river. I got the money, put on my best clothes, packed a bag, walked by Masek's dark place and through dark streets to town.

I knew what was the safest thing to do, if I could put it over. That was to high-tail it right to New York, phone her to meet me there. But there was no train due, and the station was dark and closed. If I hung around the bus station, I might be picked up any minute. That left hitchhiking. They'd be looking for that, too. I thought of a better plan as I walked, if she was willing.

I decided to phone from the station, but the station door was locked. A bar phone was dangerous, but I had to do it. It was nearly midnight and I must hurry. I didn't want to wake her. I was shaking when I dropped that dime in. What if she didn't answer? Or wasn't in town?

She was. Her voice warmed me and set me shaking in a new way. She was wonderful. She caught on right away. And when I asked if she could talk freely, she said yes. I asked her to meet me, and told her where, but to use an inconspicuous car. The way she talked, you'd have thought it was she that was on the lam, not me. "Oh, how wonderful this is!" she said. "If it's as I *hope!* I've been worried *sick!*"

I met her near the lonely dock where she had left me off that night. By the time I'd walked there along back streets, she was on her way, and I had to wait only about ten minutes. She threw herself into my arms, and cried so that she shook all over. At last we sat in the car and I told her all that had happened. She didn't say a word, just sat huddled tight against me, there in that dark car, by the lonely dock on the black water.

She didn't say a word, so I kept talking. I told her what I had planned, and felt like holding my heart tight as I waited for her to answer. I was scared to death she'd say no. Because I was asking her to take a hell of a chance. If she did it, she'd be harboring a fugitive, be an accessory after the fact, and, if and when we got caught, end up behind bars for a long rap.

I could hardly believe it when she said yes. "When can you be ready?" I said.

"Now," she said. "But I'd have to leave without much money."

That was wrong, much as I liked the sound of it. "It would draw attention. You've got servants and affairs to settle. Just drive me to New York now, and get everything cleared up. Then ..."

"Whatever you say, darling. There *are* things to settle. Running out now would look bad. But I've made a start. I've let the servants go, closed the house up, and am living at the hotel — Bayhaven House. I arranged to have phone calls switched there. That's how you got me so easily."

I'd turned the car radio on, very low, just in case. But now, for some reason, it jumped out louder, and she reached to turn it down. Right then we heard it. It was a spot news interruption of a dance-music program. It even described the bag I was carrying and the suit I wore. I knew then they'd made an inventory of everything in my house when they'd sealed it and had got to it fast after they discovered my escape. She sat there breathless, and then she turned her soft eyes on me. "They're watching the roads. You heard what they said about your wife. They think she helped you, haven't located her, and suspect she'll be driving you. So New York's out, tonight."

I was in a hell of a fix. "Shut that radio off," I said.

"Kiss me," she said. "Ah, darling! Now listen. We'll drive right down the river road. Roads leading out of town are what they'll be watching. I've still got the boat, darling. You know I'd never let that go. And it's the only pleasure I've had since they took you away from me. All alone on it thinking of you, darling. We'll be safe out there. No one will think of looking for you on the *Swallow*. She's all gassed up. I've seen to that every day. By this time tomorrow, we can be far down the Inland Waterway. No one would ever think of that, because I've let it be known I have a buyer for the boat in New York. Anyone noticing that it's gone will simply think he's bought it and sailed off."

It was the perfect solution, all right, except for one thing. Anyone noticing that *she* was gone, so suddenly gone, might tie us up. How, I couldn't see now. There was no reason for anyone to connect us. But when Rogers discovered that Chris was innocent of aiding me, sure as hell he'd *chercher* another *femme*. He still had Claire's letter to me. And, for all I knew, he might have been working on it. But I found she'd never registered to vote. "Why bother? Hobson's choice of two bums," she had said.

But there was no time to argue now. Get on that boat first; be safe. So I told her to make for it. I didn't see much of her estate because it was too dark. But it was big, the house big and white, with giant trees around it, and lawns all over. They had a small dock in the shallow water and the little dinghy was there. We went out to the *Swallow,* tied up, went into the dark cabin, and she came into my arms.

I'd been dreaming about this, visioning this moment

for days and nights in that hot cell. I forgot everything. Even the not-too-far-off scream of a siren didn't bother me. Maybe it was an ambulance, or a fire — or even the police; but I didn't care. Why should I? I was safe, and I had the woman I loved in my arms.

But, later, when my head felt cooler, warning started beating into it. She couldn't stay here. And staying out late, coming into a hotel alone, a new widow, would draw attention. Even though it was known that she spent part of each day packing and inventorying at the closed house.

"But I've already let it out I intend to go away as soon as I can. The familiar sights here, the memories upset me so. And my doctor has advised that. But first there's something I must get. You may have to help me on that. So far I've missed on it."

She didn't tell me what, and I sensed she didn't want me to ask. She hadn't mentioned her dead husband except by inference. I was tempted to ask, but something warned me not to. And warned me *never* to. I'd admitted no guilt to her, though I knew damned well she knew I'd killed Mae and Walter. And she must know that I was sure she'd killed her husband. No truer words have ever been said then: Let sleeping dogs lie. Even if you have to lie yourself. So for the rest of our lives I intended to do just that.

We hadn't used the outboard on the dinghy, because it might be heard. From the curtained windows of the cabin, I watched her row back until the little boat melted into the dark. Then I went in and listened to the turned-down radio. There was only one more reference to my escape. But it was a summary and gave me the whole picture. It was Rogers again, of course. Normally they wouldn't have missed me for hours, but the announcer said Detective Rogers had gone to my cell on unexpected business and had discovered the escape. All outlets from the city had been roadblocked immediately and an early arrest was expected. The fugitive's wife had been cleared of any complicity, having been located at a rooming house on Brook Street. She had changed residence that day to the new address.

So Chris was in with Mrs. Murphy. Maybe had Mae's old room. Apparently a beautiful friendship had developed from the night of the murder. Well, they could have each other. I had what I wanted. In a few days Claire could clean up her business, leave without causing comment.

I got into the neat bed, still warm and fragrant from her, and slept soundly until morning.

## Chapter Thirteen

About ten o'clock she came out, dressed in those red shorts and a white blouse, like the first time I saw her. She had a hamper of food for me and a big thermos of coffee. Anyone seeing her would think she was just boating for the day. To quiet her nerves, help her forget her sorrow ...

"I'm still going to the big house every day," she told me. "Cleaning up odds and ends, and most of my clothes are still there. So I'm not being noticeable. Everything else, including the furniture and cars and so on, is to be auctioned. I'm still working on the most important item, but so far, no luck." She didn't tell me what that was, either.

To make it look good, we took the boat down the river. I, of course, was out of sight in the cabin. But she had to be back early, to clean up some details with her lawyer. In the cabin I read the morning papers she had brought. It was a hell of a story, all right, but there was damned little in quotes from my lawyer or the D.A. Rogers, of course, was as full of bull as usual. Big dark hints of things he wasn't telling "at this time." Chris was the one now who was "in collapse under a doctor's care." In collapse from gin. There was nothing important on the radio, except a brief of what the papers said. But I had something more interesting to read. She'd brought me out some Florida literature, mostly about fishing places, which her husband had collected for reference.

"We can buy an island down there," she said. "One of those hundreds of little keys. But we have to have ready cash for that — lots. I'm working on that now. It may be months before the estate is settled," she gave me that loving smile, "but *we* want to be settled before that, darling."

Well, that made it; that made my dream come true. I'd have to keep under cover on the cruise down there, of course, but that would be easy. The Inland Waterway is crowded with boats like hers at this time of year. They're full of people gypsying around, and nobody pays any attention to them as long as they pay for what they buy and don't tie up to big docks and play the night spots. Once in Florida, of course, I'd have to leave her, stay under cover until she bought the island and was established there. As for leaving here, she couldn't just jump aboard and take off. Oh, no. She'd have to leave in the conventional way: take the train for New York. And then take a train *from* New York. But not to Florida. She'd go to Philadelphia, and change there for Atlantic City. I'd make the run at night, a distance of about a hundred miles, pick her up at a quiet place I knew not far from town, and *then* we'd be off for Florida.

So I daydreamed all afternoon after she left me, tied to the buoy, snug in that closed cabin. Through the window I could see the poor bastards out there working the old clam bed near the nautical-mile post. They must be hard up; there wouldn't be two baskets there. Boats went by, rocking me, and there was plenty of life on the river. But not for me; not for me any more. I was out of it. No more back-breaking clam rake, no more drunken Mae laying for me, no more gin-crying Chris. No. Now I was going to *live*. As a man like me should live. With a woman I could be proud of.

I slept on that. She woke me. It was already dark. But I wasn't hungry — not for food, just for her. Somehow that night she was more loving than ever before. She didn't say much, didn't want to talk about the trip even, so I sensed something was wrong. It scared me. Could something have come up that she was afraid to tell me? She had more ways of hearing things than radio and newspapers. She was a rich, important woman in this locality, with a lot of friends.

I didn't want to be left worrying like that, so I worked on her until at last she admitted it. But it wasn't bad; it almost made me laugh.

She said, "I didn't want to tell you. I wanted it to be a *fait accompli*. From me to you. I was going to try once more before giving up and asking for help. And also I have an awful fear of your leaving the boat. The boat's been lucky for us. But ashore ..."

"You want me to go ashore?"

She gripped my hand between hers. "It's this, Will. You know, when a man dies they seal everything up — safe-deposit boxes, things like that — until the estate is settled. He left a will, everything to me, so that's all right. But it's slow and we have to move fast, with fast money. What they don't know is that he had a safe. It's built in, well concealed in the back of a closet in his room. Once he left it open and I saw what was in it. Packs and packs of cash and loads of negotiable securities. They're mine, of course, too. But search as I would, I haven't been able to find the combination. So I started trying to force it. I broke that knob thing with an ax, and hacked and hacked, but I guess I'm just no good with tools. I sat down and cried before I came out here tonight. I so wanted to drop all that money in your lap, darling."

I didn't cry. I laughed there in the dark, and smoothed her soft head. Then I asked her to describe the safe and what tools were on the place. She didn't have to go beyond telling me that he had a "hobby shop" in the basement. Then I knew there'd be nothing to it. An electric drill would do that job, if he had enough bits for it.

It did. We went right in, I found all the tools I needed and had that safe open in less than an hour. It proved to be a rich haul. But poor, in one way, as far as she was concerned. Because in a small box, tucked far in back, I found what I'd be willing to bet was enough pure heroin to put the whole state on a jag. So I knew then. I knew he was a user, all right, and that she had lied to me. But I didn't say anything, just tossed the stuff back.

She didn't say anything, either. But she had seen me looking at it, and maybe she guessed, or maybe she didn't. If she did, she covered up well by dragging me back to the pile on the floor. "Oh, darling, look! There must be over a hundred thousand dollars."

"Why would he stash it away like that?"

Her soft eyes hardened. "We'll never know. Who cares? But he did, and you got it out, darling. And now we have our little island. Kiss me, darling!"

I kissed her. Then she shivered. "Oh, Will, I'm a little afraid. You've got to get back out there."

"Someone liable to come here? You said — "

"I know, darling. But they have watchmen. The Howells, on the next place, have one. And maybe the local police have orders to keep an eye out here."

She was right. It would be a hell of a note to be caught at this late date by some hick cop or frowzy watchman. So we hurried. We went down the wide, dark staircase, through the handsome house — a place such as I'd never been in before — and made it all right to the *Swallow*.

Before she left it was settled. I'd take off after dark the next night, be at the meeting place near Atlantic City early the next morning. She wasn't sure when she would leave, but her traveling time would be only a little over an hour to New York, an hour and a half to Philadelphia, and about the same to Atlantic City.

We couldn't miss now.

She didn't come to the boat the next day; we'd agreed on that, because we wanted no delay on her finishing up with legal matters and then leaving without any appearance of hurry. I could hardly wait to cast off from that buoy and be on my way down the river for the last time. I slept most of the day, and when I awoke I saw that the night would be fine. It would be perfect cruising down the Inland Waterway.

I got away all right. I went right down the channel, with an out-going tide. I went by all the old land: Buoy 23, the sand spit where the gulls loafed, thick as flies on molasses, by Snapper Cove, under the big Sand Point bridge, by the Outlet Islands, under the railroad bridge. Then the big pull took her, swept her between the two jetties that funneled into the sea.

The sea caught her then. I had to go outside, south for a while, then duck into the next inlet, and the rest would be all inside. I wondered that I felt a little sad. Going downriver must have done that, seeing the old landmarks for the last time. But the hell with that; so

I tried to sing, as the waves banged me, threw spray at me, and the *Swallow* raced on.

I got through all right. And this next day was going to be a fine one. It hadn't been decided whether she'd spend the night in Philadelphia or in Atlantic City. But it didn't matter. Either way she'd be able to meet me by nine o'clock. I tied up a little before eight and made a good breakfast. Where I was there were just a few cheap summer cottages, some fishing boats, and this old dock that had been abandoned. I'd used it several times when I'd worked as mate on a party boat out of Brigantine.

I could see Atlantic City in the distance. She could make it from there by taxi in fifteen minutes; a good paved road went right by the place. So all I had to do was wait. But I kept looking at the watch she had given me, a beautiful man's platinum job we'd found in the secret safe. Nine came, and no Claire. Nine-thirty, ten, ten-thirty, eleven, and still no Claire.

By eleven-thirty I simply couldn't stay on the boat. I got on the dock. I walked out so that I could see far up the road. Only a few cars had gone by; there was little traffic here.

Noon came. I couldn't eat. I was worried sick now. I didn't know what to do. We should have made some arrangements in case this happened, but we hadn't. She was a free agent and the trains and busses were running on time. We hadn't conceived of any possibility of delay.

*Where in hell was she?*

Not even a car in sight. But hell, a watched pot never boils. I told myself that, forced myself to go back in the boat and try to sleep. I knew I couldn't, but I tried. Maybe it was for the best that I did drop off, because I'd have put up a fight, probably been killed if they'd caught me awake.

A voice woke me. "All right. Get up. Keep your hands over your head."

There wasn't just the voice; there was the jab of a gun muzzle in my ribs.

They were two cops, in uniform, cops I'd never seen before. But they knew me; they knew my name. They called me by it as they put the cuffs on me, then went over the boat with a fine-tooth comb. But they didn't get a word out of me; not then, or later when they took me to the city.

Some hours later, Rogers came for me — Rogers and Trooper Kane of the state police. And two hours later I was back in my old cell. But they had new bars on it now, and a light in it you couldn't turn out.

They didn't let me see my lawyer. He was in New York, Rogers said. But I had to know. I wouldn't dare say one word in answer to their questions until I knew. One thing was on my side: Rogers was always so bursting with his own importance that he couldn't keep from boasting for long. But so far he hadn't done any boasting, and this time he might not. So I had to figure all possible angles, to work up some kind of defense.

How had they caught me? Where was Claire? Was she involved?

I had to pass Masek's cell on the way to my own. He was sitting in there stiff as a stone man, staring off into vacancy, never even glanced up as I called in to him. Had he talked? If so, what could he have told? He hadn't seen me kill anyone. But could he have lied that he had, to get himself off?

Chris could maybe have given me some information, but they wouldn't let me see her. I hoped that the fact that I had tried to escape proved to them only that I was guilty of theft of a boat and probably of the five thousand they'd found on me. But murder was what

Rogers wanted to get me for. Robbing a bank of a million dollars would be nothing compared to that.

They knew it was Claire's boat, of course. That must have been checked. But that needn't mean anything. I'd grabbed the first available boat and it just happened to be hers. And the money I had I'd withdrawn from my own bank. They could check that.

What worried me most was whether Rogers had checked with Claire about the stolen boat and recognized her as the woman who had come to my house to phone that day. But even if he had, it could have been just a coincidence.

They'd hammered at me as to where I'd hidden out and where I'd stolen the five thousand. I told them nothing. Rogers knew me by now and after his first work on me in Atlantic City and all the way back in the police car, he realized I wasn't going to break. So, after a preliminary report and a lot of preening, he ducked out and left me to the D.A. and the others.

But that's where Rogers was dangerous. That's what I was worried about after they put me in the cell for the night. Rogers' manner with suspects antagonized them, especially me. But when he was out digging up dirt, he was hard to beat.

And that's just what Rogers had been doing since he'd ducked out at five o'clock. I knew that the minute I saw his eyes as they let him into my cell after midnight. Outside he had handed his gun to the turnkey and said, "I don't want any snooping around here. Keep everybody away, no matter who. Don't worry, I can take care of myself with that half-wit clam digger."

I got off the pallet and I gave him back his look. "Not if you didn't have a whole police force to back you up," I said. "Not if we were alone where you couldn't call for help."

"You'll be calling for help before I'm through with you, Peters," and as he said it he looked down into his hand. There was a watch there, and he studied it carefully, frowning. "In just about one minute," he said. "By the watch."

He let me see it then. It was the watch they had taken from me when I was arrested. It was the watch Claire and I had found in that safe and that she had given to me. Well, to the victor belong the spoils. Maybe he had some of my five thousand, too.

"You'll have to work faster than you've shown so far," I said. "None of your flannel-mouthing up to date has got you anywhere."

"Not with you, because you're a half-wit, Peters. Logic is wasted on you."

"Why try, then?"

"But not wasted on others."

"It was wasted on Chris. On Masek. Who've you been wasting it on now?"

He smiled then. It was an evil smile. "Wrong on both counts, Peters."

He turned the watch over in his hand. "A pretty watch, isn't it? Expensive, too. Solid platinum, finest Swiss movement."

"Where did you steal it?" No use showing him I recognized it.

He smiled again. "Where did *you* steal it, Peters?"

I was still smiling when he thumbnailed the back open, held the shining inner case out where I could read what was Written on it. It read: "Dixon Grace. Individual winner, International Tuna Club, 1947."

My smile went then. That watch came from the same place as that stolen red boat. Claire was getting closer and closer now. But where was she? What had happened to her?

"Well, Peters?"

"Well, what?"

"Quit your stalling. You were in possession of Grace's boat and watch. Why that particular person, Peters?"

"You tell me. People sometimes leave watches on boats."

"By God, I will tell you! You remember that day she came to your house? Said she wanted to use the phone?"

"Who?"

"You know who. And *I* know who, *now.*"

"You're talking in riddles."

"I could have been. But not now. Not since I learned that she stopped that red boat off Masek's place and asked where you lived. Asked by *name,* Peters. And that was some two hours before I saw her in your front room. And during those two hours her boat was tied up to your dock."

"Not that I know of."

"That kind of talk won't get you anywhere; not with the evidence that she asked for you by name, and then, in my presence, acted as though you were a stranger."

"Lots of people ask for me by name. People who like fresh-out-of-the-water clams, and have heard I dig them."

He looked at me for a long, long moment, his eyes greedy and hating, and then he said, very softly, "Maybe. But lots of them don't lose a husband by sudden death at the same time that you knock off your common-law wife. No matter how much they love clams, Peters."

I went cold then. He was really on the trail. He was showing his hand because he thought it was unbeatable. But one thing I mustn't forget — the advice that old lawyer had given Braden when he started out to practice law: Admit nothing, deny everything.

I'd beat him.

"Go on," I said, "if it makes you happy. Or makes sense to you. None of it does to me."

"I'll do that," he said. "You once told me, Peters, that your memory is excellent. So you must remember that love note that almost, but not quite, sank you. Until your romantic nuptials."

I laughed. "Oh, sure," I said. "I remember a phony letter I assumed you had some dame write, Rogers. In order to make Chris jealous and tell your lies. But that hat trick is old hat now."

"Yeah?" His eyes gleamed. Apparently I'd cued him just right. He said, "In spite of that, I kept the letter, Peters. And when I questioned Mrs. Grace about her boat and asked her to identify this watch, she had to sign some routine stuff. I saw that. So, if I had some dame write that love letter, Peters, it must have been Mrs. Dixon Grace. I didn't need a fingerprint expert to tell me it was the same handwriting. But later, in court, of course, that will be necessary routine."

He sat back on that and watched me with the eye of a hunter sure of his game. Claire must have been at headquarters today. She had been questioned. Rogers knew she had asked for me by name that day in the boat. So Masek had talked. And there was little doubt that Rogers had gone to Chris today, told her that I was planning to take it on the lam with Claire Grace, the hell with her and our marriage.

Rogers was sure of himself, sure he was right in at the kill, but he played it easy. He said, "Peters, I take back that you're a half-wit. I get mad and talk that way sometimes, As a matter of fact, you're a damned smart cookie. What I haven't been able to figure out is why an intelligent, good-looking man like you could ever have got mixed up with that Hunt woman. Chris

I could understand. But hell, with a woman like Mrs. Grace on your list, that doesn't make sense either. Now it all adds up to this: how you feel about Mrs. Grace. Her letter seems to show how she feels about you."

"What difference would it make how I feel? Assuming I even know the woman."

He leaned toward me then and lowered his voice to a whisper. "This difference, Peters. So far, nobody knows all that I know. That letter I took from your mailbox — it's not a matter of record, and hasn't been out of my possession. But it's the key to more than your guilt in the Hunt matter. It could instigate an exhumation order that might show a different story as to how Dixon Grace died. Even if they found no evidence of foul play on an autopsy, you and Mrs. Grace would share a hell of a lot of newspaper space, Peters. Not that you'd give a damn, maybe, assuming that she was just another dame to you. But it would ruin her. She'd be named as an accessory, at least, after the fact; because your being caught with her boat and her husband's watch indicates collusion rather than theft. Her letter to you would tie that up. And when your wife learns that, she'll talk. She can't be forced to testify against her husband, but she can *volunteer* to. And she *will*. I know the type."

Of all he had said, the thing that burned me most was "Not that you'd give a damn, maybe, assuming that she was just another dame to you." That I couldn't take. That wasn't true. Not if he answered my next question the way I hoped and prayed he would. I asked it. "One thing I have to know before I'll say a word. I want it true. Is your word good, Rogers?"

The way he answered reassured me. Another matter of ego with him. He jumped at it. "I've pulled some fast ones in my time, Peters. Gone over the edge once or twice because of overenthusiasm. Like what I did that got me demoted — I helped a relative out on a deal that turned out to be shady. But when I was questioned I told the truth. The Chief knows that, and everyone on the force. They demoted me instead of kicking me out for that very reason. My word is known to be good."

"I'll accept it, then. Who talked to Mrs. Grace when she was here today?"

"I did all the questioning. But it wasn't here. It was at the Bayhaven Hospital."

*"Hospital?"* My heart seemed to stop.

He noticed the shock, had been waiting for it. He said casually, "Yeah."

"You mean she's sick? Hurt?"

"A funny thing, Peters. It seems she was all packed for a trip to New England. To recuperate from the shock of her beloved husband's sudden death. The taxi that was taking her to the train for New York got hit on Route Thirty-five by a drunk driver. A damned bad smash, but she came out of it alive, though it killed her driver. Someone must have had her by the hand. Fate, maybe, preserving her for ..." he shrugged. "Anyway, that beautiful face of hers was unmarred. So I had no difficulty in recognizing her as the woman who said she wanted to use your phone."

"Did she recognize you?"

"Funny thing, she did. She was very nice and cooperative. Except that she said she'd never heard of you, Peters. I thought that was odd, since she'd asked Masek for you by name that day, but I didn't comment on it. And another funny thing: she was unconscious when they took her to the hospital. Naturally, they looked through her bags for identification and so on. You know what they found, Peters? Over a hundred thousand bucks in cash and securities. And you know another thing? My checking turned up that you'd drawn those five thousand bucks we found on you from your bank, as you insisted you had. Cleaned out your account. Also that you'd made a deal to sell your house. Your minds must have been running in the same channel, Peters."

My mind was dead right then. He had me. He had the big stuff. The rest was chicken feed. But I was entitled to that. I said, "All right, let's cut the cute irony, Rogers. You've made your point. Don't labor it. Is she hurt badly?"

"They only let me see her a few minutes. I assume not, though."

"All right, what do you want?"

"You know what I want, Peters. I want a confession right now that you killed Mae and Walter Hunt. Give me that and I'll give you your love letter. You can burn it right here. That's the only positive link between you and Mrs. Dixon Grace that would stand up in court. And I'm not interested in Mrs. Grace. I set out to prove that you did murder, and I'll settle for that. If the Bayhaven police want to explore her activities, that's up to them."

"Have they any reason to?"

"Not that I know of. And they won't have anything from me if you confess, Peters."

"Have you told any of this to Chris?"

"I've told it to no one. And I won't."

"What about Masek saying she asked for me by name?"

"I didn't say he did. That lie of yours about kids breaking your window with stones boomeranged. But like a good cop, I had to check it. I located a little colored kid who happened to be in the high grass nearby, fishing. He heard her ask Masek where you lived. He said the sea gull answered. Thought that was very funny. But he's forgotten it by now and hasn't told anyone else. Because I handled it that way. This is going to be a hundred-percent Rogers job, Peters."

No doubt of it. And that I hated. But what could I do? The one big thing, the thing that made me almost happy, was the fact that she hadn't run out on me. That fear had been gnawing at me, but now I could take anything. She had been on her way to me when her taxi got hit. Full of love, she had been rushing to me. Right now she was covering up for me. She was true blue.

I knew he'd answer anything now because he saw I was breaking. So I asked him, "How did they pick me up the way they did?"

"A kid at that dock near Atlantic City told his father about the swell red boat and the funny name on it. They were at lunch and the radio was on — news bulletin about your escape in a Bayhaven boat named the *Swallow*. So he phoned the Atlantic City police."

"I mean how did the news get out?"

"Oh. That's a funny one, Peters. You know a man named Andy Love? Clam-digger, like yourself? The one who raked up Walter Hunt's body?"

I knew the sonofabitch. He was one of those clam pirates who made it hard for an honest digger to make a living. They tear hell out of clam beds with outboard motors, churn every damned clam in sight up, kill the beds. It's illegal, but they do it in the dark on low tides, use lookouts, and get away with it. It gives the rest of us a bad name.

Rogers was saying, almost pleasantly, "Yeah. I worked him over pretty hard after he found Hunt's body. I knew the sonofabitch was lying, and he knew I did. Because there wasn't a cent of all that money Hunt had collected for the laundry. Just an empty billfold. Love ghouled that money off the body, of course. Because your killing was motivated by hate, not by money."

"You mean Love beat you to it." I couldn't help saying it.

He gave me a dirty laugh. "You should condone him! In a way, he's what they call your nemesis, Peters. He doesn't like you because you bounced one off his chin once for bumping your boat. And he's had an eye out for that Grace woman, bare legs and all, racing downriver in that fancy red boat. My guess is, he got a load of rotgut in him and took a peek in her buoyed boat, maybe to try and make a little time with her. That was late afternoon, and he saw you asleep through the cabin window. But by the time he got the news to me — wanting a reward and to soft-soap me — you'd taken off. It was a dark night and the Coast Guard didn't spot you, because we thought you'd made for New York."

So that was that. But I knew I'd never get a chance to bounce another one off the chin of that bastard Andy Love. Rogers had been watching me almost happily, and before I spoke he knew it was in the bag for him. I said:

"Your word you'll leave her out of this completely? Even after they finish with me?"

He said, "My word of honor, Peters." He said it almost piously. But I believed him. I knew him. Claire Grace was rich, had rich friends, and the Bayhaven authorities wouldn't like being shown up by a two-bit detective from another town. In the end it might mean his own ruin. And he'd made his kill.

"Give me the letter," I said.

"When you've dictated and signed that confession, Peters."

"I like my word better than yours, Rogers."

We eyed each other hard there, for a long time. Then

I broke. I had to break. To get me, he'd drag even the biggest shot in America into a dirty court. And he had the evidence to ruin her. That I couldn't take. Not thinking of her lying there in a hospital, probably in pain, but not giving an inch. She hadn't let me down. I wouldn't let her down.

"All right, Rogers," I said. "I'll give it to you."

## Chapter Fourteen

I kept leaning forward in the taxi, like a jockey on a lagging horse, as though trying to urge it on. The cab seemed to be just crawling. It certainly wasn't keeping pace with my feverish mind. That was a mixture of elation and a deep, hounding foreboding. Elation because soon I'd see Claire Grace, foreboding because I knew Rogers would move heaven and earth to nullify my lucky break.

That break was: I was out on a writ of habeas corpus. The whole thing happened like a bolt out of the blue. I was just finishing my confession, which Rogers had let me write in my cell because there was no stenographer available at that time of night, and probably for other reasons of his own, when it happened.

Luckily, Rogers was asleep upstairs, because I'd warned him it would be a long and carefully written job. The turnkey on duty was an old-woman type, a political pensioner. He lost his head when, on his rounds, he flashed his light into Masek's cell and found him hanging from the window bars, a noose made from his trousers around his neck. He dashed in there, yelling. I was the only one awake. In his excitement he showed me the paper, headed in big, black penciled letters: "CONFESSION." "Look at this! Look at this!"

he was chattering. Under the blocked word "confession" Masek had written, also in block letters, "I KILLED WALTER HUNT."

Luckily, other prisoners woke up then, and the head jailer got on the job before Rogers knew about it, or there probably would have been another confession burned. Because I burned mine then and there.

Later, when Braden arrived on the scene, I learned what was in that confession of Masek's. It was damned clever. Apparently he'd known about the time elements concerned. He'd been up, all right, and had seen and heard plenty. Including the exact time Rogers, Mrs. Murphy, and Chris had left my house that night. Right after they had gone, his confession said, he heard loud voices and a fight going on near his shack. He went out to protest. He said he saw Mae threatening Walter with a pistol and Walter accusing her of being on her way to my house. He said he'd been hiding, waiting to catch her. Walter knocked the gun from her hand, throttled her, and then attacked him. But Masek got to the gun on the ground and shot Walter. Because he, himself, was wanted for a murder in Michigan, he feared to report to the police. He had simply tossed them both into the river, with the gun in Walter's pocket.

He went on to say that he'd thought since I was innocent, I'd get off all right. But when I'd escaped from the jail, he knew that would indicate that I was guilty to the police. And then he'd heard they had checked his fingerprints and had him for the Michigan killing anyway, so he might as well confess this.

But why did he hang himself? Braden told me the answer to that. He'd gone out to the animal pound for Masek's dog and cat. He swore there was a sea gull, a big gray one, perched on a post of the runway. Maybe it was Wilbur, and maybe it wasn't. The point was that Masek's dog and cat had been 'put to sleep' by order of Rogers. That was the biggest mistake Rogers ever made. Braden had sensed that and laid it on thick to Masek, to add to his hate of Rogers and make sure that Masek would never give him any useful evidence. It had worked better than he had hoped.

"Though I'm not putting it that way," Braden told me. "I feel sorry as hell for the poor old man. You know how he ended that confession? He wrote: 'With the little fellows gone, I have nothing to live for. All I hope is that I go to animal heaven — or hell, for that matter — so I can be with them. I've had enough of humans.' And I imagine that wife of his he killed was worse than your Mae. He confided in me that she wouldn't let him keep a pet in the house. He defied her, brought a broken-winged crow in. She broke its neck with a broom, and he broke hers with a baseball bat."

Poor Masek. But hell, he was better off. He had nothing to live for. But I had. Every tick of that taxi meter was taking me closer to her. But something also kept hitting me in the head. It seemed to make my head tick. I'd been through a lot in the past days, and my head had been aching like hell. Probably because I never had to use it much, and lately I'd overworked it.

But now it had to work right. Rogers had that letter of Claire's. Nothing would stop him now. And he knew just how to do it — ruin Claire Grace. He'd pull down the whole world to hurt me. I hadn't seen hide or hair of him since they'd released me. And even then he didn't say a word to me. He just gave me a look that left no doubt in my mind. Because when he'd tried to tell them I'd confessed and had started to write it out, I said he was a liar.

Chris had said a word. She had said so many and so

fast, at the jail, that the gin smell sickened me. She was maudlin, slobbering all over me, telling me how wonderful it was going to be from now on. She was so drunk that Mrs. Murphy, who was with her, took my tip and got her back to her room. I'd be there when I finished my business with my lawyer, I told her.

I was out on bail. They'd accepted my five thousand for that. And I told Braden that I'd see Dr. Algee as soon as I could. Because he'd told me the doctor wanted to see me, but hadn't wanted to bother me at the jail or interrupt my reunion with my wife.

Wife, hell. My big worry now was: when would Claire be out of the hospital? Rogers hadn't seemed to know just how seriously she was hurt, but he'd given me the impression it wasn't bad. I had to see her. They couldn't keep me from doing that if I gave a phony name and said I was from her lawyer's office. Because, sure as hell, she could sue that drunk driver.

Not that she would. We didn't want any more legal hassles. What I had to do was tell her about that letter Rogers had, warn her to admit nothing, deny everything; and better yet, play real sick so she couldn't see anyone. Not even the important Mr. Rogers.

I'd have to jump bail. But hell, it was my own money I was giving them, wasn't it? And cheap at twice the price. She could join me later. She could just walk out of the hospital and be on her way before Rogers even had a hint she was able to be up and around.

He'd have to find us before he could do anything. There wouldn't be any big red boat to look for this time. And she still had that hundred thousand dollars.

I was thinking that as the cab turned into the drive to the white brick hospital that fronted on the river. I got out in the parking place and dismissed the driver. I hoped they'd let me sit with her a long time. Another car stopped behind the taxi, but I didn't pay any attention to that. Some guy probably coming to see an old bag of a wife just out of a sense of duty.

At the desk downstairs, the receptionist gave me a funny look when I said my phony name and told her who I wanted to see. "Are you a friend? A close friend?"

I told her I was. It was probably too late for regular visiting hours, so I was about to explain it was important business, too; but she turned away and was talking softly into a telephone.

I've never remembered in detail just what happened after that. But I was in a small reception room and this nurse was there, and I was staring at her, not able, to think or speak or move. But I'll never forget one thing she said. She said, "I was with her right to the end. When the operation failed and she knew she was going to die, she said you'd come and she wanted you to know what she said. I'll never forget it, because she looked so beautiful and her voice was quite clear. As though talking to you, not me. She said. 'I'll see you there, darling. Soon, I think.' Then she died, poor child."

She wasn't there now; not at the hospital. She was at a mortuary in the town. I didn't know what to do, because my mind wouldn't work. My head seemed just like an empty shell. There didn't seem to be any breath in me, any heart in me, any blood. The nurse reached for me, tried to give me something, but I must have brushed her away. Because the next thing I remember, there was Rogers. Or maybe I was imagining him. I must have been, because normally I'd have needed nothing more than that hard smug face gloating over me. I'd have killed him with my bare hands, gun or not.

But I didn't do that. I just stood and stared at that ghost of a Rogers. But I remember what it said. It said. "She missed on that, Peters. It's Masek she'll see. You know, funny thing, in a death like this they usually rat on each other. The woman *always* does. I guess this is the exception that proves the rule. And I want you to know I didn't guess she was hurt that bad. She sure was a good-looking woman. And she wrote a nice hand. You should keep this to remember her by."

He was holding something out to me. It was the love letter Claire Grace had sent to me, with the envelope clipped to it. I didn't hit him. I didn't even want to. He was the only one in the world who knew how I felt and why I felt that way. And besides, he didn't look smug now. He didn't look mean. He looked sorry as hell for me. And he must have told the nurse to phone for Dr. Algee, fearing that no one else in that hospital, including him, could handle me now.

But I was like a lamb. Or maybe I was just that way because of what Dr. Algee shot into me. Because I dreamed away in that hospital room, almost pleasant dreams, always seeing Claire Grace's face smiling at me, a beckoning smile. I saw other things, too, because I wasn't asleep. I was holding onto a sort of semi-consciousness that, oddly, made my thoughts very definite and clear. Some of it came from Dr. Algee; soothing talk to me before he left. "Everything is going to be all right from now on, Will. Mr. Rogers tells me you're entirely in the clear on that Hunt matter. I've had quite a talk with him and he has an amazing understanding of you. I'll provide the rest. I'll tell you about that tomorrow, after you've had a good sleep. You've been through a bad time, but remember, it's an ill wind that blows no good. You'll see what I mean later. Right now, just remember that you're among friends. And you have a nice wife, and a family on the way. Just keep that in mind, Will."

I was keeping it in mind. I was thinking about what

Rogers had said: "She missed on that ... It's Masek she'll see." But she hadn't missed, any more than she'd missed on anything she'd done before she died. Because I knew one thing: I could never live with Chris. The way she'd acted at the jail when they released me, drunk as she was, made me sure there'd be no running out on her. No more chance of that than there'd been with Mae Hunt. In the end, she'd be another Mae. And her kid would be another Walter Hunt. Even if Claire hadn't been up there waiting for me, I'd have had to do the same thing. But she *was* waiting for me. Didn't she tell the nurse that?

No, crime certainly wouldn't pay under the conditions so soothingly painted by Dr. Algee. I'd be freer and happier in prison. Even in the nut house. But there was something I could do. It made me happy to think about it. I could almost catch up with Claire. Because I'm sure there's a place where people like us go after death. Unhappy people who have done wrong, but who can be rehabilitated. But together. Like Alcoholics Anonymous.

But I couldn't do it here; not tonight. There wasn't a thing in the bare room to do it with. Tomorrow was time enough. And I wanted to be absolutely sure. So I'd play humble and thankful and agree with everything Dr. Algee said. All I'd need was a few minutes alone in my own house. My five thousand bail money and the property would go to Chris. She'd drink it up in a year, but she was entitled to that. She was my legal wife, wasn't she?

Funny, I went off on that thought. And, funnier yet, when I came fully awake the next day, she was standing by my bed. And still funnier yet, she wasn't reeking of gin. Her face was very pale, but she looked presentable enough. Her hair was fixed up nice, and she had on a new, neat little suit.

She put on a good act before the nurse, kissing and fussing over me. I realized from what she said that all they'd told her was that I'd had a nervous breakdown and they'd brought me here to the hospital.

But that wasn't all. What she told me next scared me. Somehow I had to lick that. Because I'd expected they'd turn me loose. Then I could go back home and get set for what I had to do. I didn't want to mess myself up with a gun. Claire had gone with her face still beautiful. And I couldn't drown myself, any more than a seal can. So it had to be gas. I used the bottled kind in my cook stove, and I could seal my little kitchen tight. I'd write my will out first, and then I'd do that.

But now here was that slobbering Chris, and what she told me scared me. She said, "Dr. Algee sent for me because he says it ain't nothing to get sceered of, but they gotta send for a man's wife when they operate in any hospital."

"Operate for what, for God's sake? On my nerves?"

"Yes, hon. Now don't get excited. I'll be right here all the time. They jest gonna give you a nice X-ray and things like that and then, if it's like he thinks, Dr. Algee's jest gonna make a little operation on your head. And you know what, hon? He's got another doctor coming from New York to help him. He got some famous cases in the papers. Rogers told me about one. A guy was in Sing Sing for vicious, brutal murdering of six, seven people, including his own father and mother and his mother-in-law. You know what this doctor done? Rogers said he jest cut a coupla nerves in this con's brain, and now the guy's home, happily married, and head of the school board."

Happily married and head of the school board.

I was just about to curse hell out of her, run her out of there, when Dr. Algee came in with this

Frankenstein of a surgeon. I didn't have to let them cut me. And that moron Chris had no right to give her consent. I wanted to get out of here and fast. But I'd never do it by yelling at them; give them a chance to say I was nuts and put me in a strait jacket. So I played it cagey. My idea was to act scared, stall for time. I said:

"Is this operation dangerous, Doctor?"

They looked at each other and the strange doctor nodded to Dr. Algee. "Yes, Will," he said. "A major brain operation is always a gamble."

"I don't have to take it if I don't want to?"

"No. Of course not. But I must tell you this: What you've been through lately has given that condition of yours a turn for the worse. I fear it will become progressively so. Dr. Neelman, here, after what I've told him, thinks so too. He's had great experience in this line."

"You mean with criminals, though. Cutting into their brains."

They didn't get sore. They looked very mild and soothing. "Now, now, Will! Don't get upset," Dr. Algee said. "A brain's a brain, you know. Dr. Neelman has proved pretty well there's no such thing as a criminal brain, per se. But a brain can become affected to such an extent that it tolerates criminal acts, even forces them. It could happen to you. Of course, you have the right to refuse to be operated on. But you should consider the alternative, Will."

"What's the alternative?"

"Indefinite observation and treatment in an indicated hospital."

"A nut house, you mean. They can't make me go there."

"Yes, Will, they can."

They could, too. I guessed that by the way Dr. Algee's

eyes had hardened. He was a kind man, very gentle and quiet. But there was a steel there I hadn't suspected, and now it was showing. And I guessed why. Rogers had transferred some of that "amazing understanding" of me to Dr. Algee. He knew I was guilty and had told Dr. Algee that, and they'd both agreed that my wound was to blame.

All right, so be it. Rogers had won again. And another thing added to my decision; made it, probably. It was a dangerous operation. There was a good chance I'd die on the operating table. And where was I? Why, in the Bayhaven Hospital, maybe even in the same room where Claire had lived her last moments. And they'd do it in the same room where they'd operated on Claire. On the same table.

That would be the perfect way to go. I'd pray for it before I went under the anesthetic. But if I missed, I'd still have my own anesthetic waiting in the gas bottle by the river.

"Okay, go ahead," I said.

I didn't die on the table. But I might as well have died, because for a long, long while I didn't know I was alive. I was just a body, no mind. I might just as well have been someone else's body, for all I knew.

They told me later how long I was just a body. It seemed incredible that a man could eat and sleep and do all the other bodily things, and not know a thing about it. But I must have done those things. Or had them done for me. But I remember when I first came to, when I could see and barely think a little. My first impression was of the hissing and banging of the steam radiator in my room.

So it was winter. And I was in this strange room. And it was night, because a small light was on. I lay there letting thoughts seep quietly into my mind. Into my brain. I didn't think of it in that way at first. I didn't remember what had happened. I didn't even know who I was. All I knew was that I was alive; I was alive like a newborn baby. Maybe *they* think when they're first born. Nobody will ever know. Maybe they thought as I was thinking; just tiny little wisps of thought, inspired by what I saw about me in that little room.

But it seemed like a big, important place to me.

And then it grew smaller. Day by day it grew smaller. At first I didn't know who Dr. Algee was; but, bit by bit, very patiently, he brought little things back to me. He was the only one who saw me, except the nurse, and she only said a few pleasant words to me, impersonal words, probably on his instructions.

I was doing fine, he told me one day; and that day he explained about the operation, and told me not to strain to remember all that had happened. It didn't matter. Not at this time, all at once. But in the long run it did matter. What I must do was let nature do it for me. A sort of mental gravity. And when things finally all fell into place, he'd know the operation had been successful.

Funny, I'd gained weight. I felt like a slob there in that bed, with that slip of a nurse doing everything for me, treating me like a baby. She never had said anything personal, but I wondered if I'd been delirious, maybe had said things she'd heard that would jog my memory. So I asked her. But she said no. Things began coming back, though. Claire came back. She came back like a sudden flash of light, and then it was easy.

It was late at night and I was alone in the room, supposedly asleep. But I'd had this dream. It was a wild one, of a sinking red boat in a raging sea, and this woman was in my arms with long blonde hair getting in my eyes and throttling me so I couldn't swim and save her. And I was calling her Claire.

I woke up with sweat, and I lay there shaking as the whole thing came back to me. It was like watching a horror movie. It started right in with me throttling Mae and ended right in this hospital with Chris slobbering over me and Dr. Algee explaining the operation.

I was right back where I'd been then.

I didn't want to be back there. I cursed Dr. Algee, and I cursed Chris, and I cursed myself. Dr. Algee had tried to help me and he had ruined me. If he'd kept out of it, long ago I'd have been on my way to join Claire. I'd have joined her, hard and muscled and tanned. I'd have been beautiful, the way she was.

But now look at me! Shaking, I threw the clothes from me, ripped my pajamas off. Look at me! I was fish-belly white, pimpled, flabby. If it hadn't been for the way I looked, I'd have jumped out the window, or strangled myself with a sheet. No nurse was there to give an alarm.

I cried then. I cried and cried, and the nurse must have heard, because she came running in, and I heard her call for an orderly. But he wasn't needed. She was small, but she'd been good to me. I couldn't hurt her. So I let her put the needle in and it did the trick. I slept again.

The next day Dr. Algee came. The nurse had told him, of course, and I did, too. It didn't seem to bother him. He even seemed pleased. I told him that I'd remembered everything, but what had set me off was remembering how I'd looked before, and now I was like some slob who worked at a desk all day.

"You've said I'm all right physically," I told him. "And now my mind is clear. Why can't I leave here? Get back into shape? I'm ashamed of myself."

I noticed the change in his eyes as I said that last sentence. "Ashamed of yourself, Will? You really feel that way?"

"Yes," I said. "You know how I looked before. I can't stand to look at myself now. But a few months on the river and I'd be back in shape. Living in my own house and all. I'm homesick, Doctor."

He was watching me carefully. He said quietly, "Does that include your wife, Will? Do you miss her?"

I knew that was a trick question, so I said yes, I did. And he said, "We haven't let her come because I wanted it to be a gentle and gradual desire on your part. But she's been here every day. With flowers and little things she's made for you, cooked for you. The nurse told you that, but it didn't register of course."

"No, but now it does. The only thing, sudden like this, a man knowing he's married ... I mean, if I could just go home. Be alone there for awhile, until I get adjusted. I've lived there alone so long ..."

"Yes, that's understandable. But alone, this soon. Will ... I wouldn't advise it. And your wife is living in your house now. That is as it should be, of course. And she'll be delivered in April — only three months from now."

Hearing those words brought out sweat all over me. She was living there. *In my house.* And I was here in this hospital, where, if I had any new blow-up, they've have more excuse for delaying my release. I had to get out of here, even if it meant going back to live in that house with Chris. It was the lesser of two evils. But I didn't tell him that, I played it cagey.

I played it this way: I waited two days, and during those days I talked to the nurse about my loving wife. I moped over the flowers she had sent, the snapper soup — not as good as Mae's, but not bad — and I said I was lonely as hell.

It worked like a charm. She passed it on to Dr. Algee, all right, and it pleased him. He let Chris come and see me. She was pretty swelled up by now, looked in worse shape than me. But I told her she looked swell, kissed her time and time again, and she bawled all over me. There wasn't a whiff of gin from her.

"The doctor said I mustn't drink, not while I'm carrying the little one, hon. But you know sump'n? I don't even miss it. I got *him* now. He takes the place of it. Him and dreaming of you coming home soon now, hon. I ast Dr. Algee, and you know how he sometimes kids? Like him saying, 'It's hard to say no to a beautiful girl like you, Mrs. Peters. If he keeps on improving like he's been, he'll be home soon. If you promise to take good care of him.' Oh, hon, will I take good care of you! Jest you wait and see!"

I didn't have to wait long after that. I'll never forget stepping through that door. She had the place fixed up really nice. But there was one thing she had done that I couldn't have figured. That was bad. She was very proud of it. "They let me have the bail money," she said. "Oh, I wanted to surprise you, hon! So I went and threw that ugly gas stove out and put in this lovely electric one. Ain't it handsome, sweet?"

It was handsome, but you couldn't seal the room up, turn it on, and drift off to join Claire Grace with it.

Not only had she bought the stove, but she'd got new aluminum windows, storm and screen. They did make the place less drafty, snugger when the river wind hit from the north. And she'd bought a raft of cookbooks. She cooked by print, but it wasn't bad, once she knew what I liked.

Algee wouldn't let me on the river. No boats, he said. Not yet. But the hell with him. I had to pull the boats up, put some sealer on them, and do a paint job. I cleaned my rakes up, timed the outboard. Not that I'd be clamming for long. Just long enough to get my muscles back where they'd been, and lots of sun on me, so I'd be looking good when I saw Claire Grace.

I knew one thing: I would have to get in perfect shape before Chris had Walter Hunt's bastard.

Rogers came in to see us once in a while. It might have been an act, but he was always pleasant, never mentioned what had gone before.

Chris had done another thing. She explained it this way: "That poor old Mr. Masek. You know, hon, the only one weeps for him is that old sea gull. And I know you won't mind, hon, but I couldn't have Mr. Masek put away in potter's field. So I used some of that money to have him put in Memorial, with a nice headstone and all. Mr. Martinello — you know, the judge's father, the stonemason — he went and carved the cat and dog and sea gull on it. Wouldn't take a cent for it."

"They were buried with him?"

"I seen to that, yes, hon. Mr. Rogers got their little bodies from the pound and was very nice."

I wondered if the sea gull, Wilbur, had a thought on his premature epitaph, but I didn't mention that to her. She'd be too dumb to know what I meant. But I went to the grave with some flowers; and then I thought, since I was there, and Hunt's father had buried Mae and Walter there, I might as well put some flowers on their graves too. It was snowing, very cold out there, with the wind from the river. There was ice on the river, but it had been warm when they'd gone into it. Thinking that made me cry. I just stood there crying. I didn't know how I got home. But she had a good dinner waiting, so I felt better and had a good sleep.

I had no desire to seek out Claire Grace's grave. She wasn't dead the way Mae and Walter were. She wasn't just moldering bones in a snowy graveyard. She was alive, and beautiful, and anxious about me. So I had to get in shape; I had to do it before that Hunt kid was born.

But I couldn't do it. I got fatter and fatter. I got to over two hundred. I knew I ought to cut down on my food, chop wood, get down the river with my rake. Every day I'd decide this was the one to begin. But I'd look out of the cozy room onto the icy river, see the rushes across the river bend hard in the north wind, and then there she'd be with an eggnog in her hand. "Come on, hon. Drink this like a good boy. Then read your nice book I got you from the Circulating. You can't go out on no river a day like this."

I'd give in. I'd give in easily. I'd read the books. What they call "escape" stories. They kept my mind off myself, off Chris and that growing belly of hers. Well, when the sun came back, in the spring, I'd get at it. I'd make up for lost time. I read till finally I got sick of it. All that implausible stuff. Hell, none of it was as exciting as what I'd been through. Truth sure was stranger than fiction. I stopped looking at TV for the same reason. So I started to write my own story. First, just for the hell of it. It kept me busy and made me feel important. Because now it came to me that, to other people, I was just a harmless fat man, married to a woman getting fatter and fatter. The hell with that. I'd done something big. I'd killed two people and got away with it. I'd influenced a beautiful woman to kill her husband for love of me. I wasn't just some white-bellied slob, eating all day and sleeping like a fat baby at night.

I was a killer.

So I wrote it all. I enjoyed it. It came easy. And it was true. Chris thought I was writing a novel and she reacted to it as you'd expect. "Like I always said, hon, you ain't just some ignorant clam digger. You got brains. And you're educated nice. You talk nice. And you think nice. So whyn't you leave everybody know it?" She even started to tell me a plot, but I said I had one. And I kept it locked up as it grew into a thicker pile day after day. I told her I wanted to surprise her with — as Claire once said — a *fait accompli.*

Saying that gave me my final idea. It was a shame to let this story die with me. I'd get it to Dr. Algee just before I shot myself downriver in my boat. Because that's what I'd have to do now. But I could do it in the heart; that wouldn't disfigure me.

Rogers knew. And Dr. Algee knew. If they hadn't talked yet, they wouldn't now. And I owed the whole true story to Dr. Algee. It might help him professionally. He thought his operation had been a great success. That, though I'd remembered all that had happened, I could now judge it as the acts of another man, a man I'd ceased to be. Now he could check back on what he had done wrong in that operation, correct it so the next one would succeed.

As I wrote, I relived the whole thing, scene by scene. And I gained weight day by day. It got so I didn't dare get on the bathroom scales; but I couldn't help eating. And she kept pouring it on.

"The doctor said I should feed you good, hon. You gotta get back your stren'th. You gotta eat like a bear does before he hydronates. Because when I go to the hospital I know you ain't going to eat right. So this will carry you through."

A hibernating bear.

I probably looked like one. Because I'd quit shaving, ashamed to look at my big blob of a face. I could write all right. My mind was clear as a bell, my memory even better than before. But when I walked, I shook the house. I hated even to walk the short distance to the bathroom. I'd breathe like a porpoise, just doing that. And then suddenly, one day, I couldn't do it. I tried, but my legs just weren't there. I fell with a crash, and heard Chris scream. Then I went out ...

It was summer when they brought me back from the hospital the second time. The weeping willows were full and green, and the marsh weeds had a new suit of clothes on. I can still use my hands enough to write, and I can move my head a little. I can move it enough to follow the boats going downriver from the wheel chair on the front porch that Chris had put up. It'll be glassed in for the winter, so I can sit and look at the river and Wilbur the gull, sitting all day on his snag within talking distance. Though he never says a word now.

I'm paralyzed everywhere else. Always will be. Dr. Algee was honest enough to tell me that. What it was, nobody seems to know. Or they wouldn't tell me. But it doesn't matter. It could be worse. I could be dead. And if I'd died looking the way I looked, no angel of heaven or hell or purgatory would have given me a friendly look. Claire would have been mortified, as Walter would have put it.

But here I get friendly looks. My little son grins and grins at me. He's in the handsome crib Rogers presented, and he gurgles away, happy as a clam at high tide. He knows me, all right. He knows I'm his daddy. He's always going to know it, because I've come to love the little fellow.

I can wheel around enough to baby-sit with him. We've become great pals. Because Chris is away a lot. As she said, somebody has to bring in the money. Rogers got her a nice job. His brother-in-law is back in business again, renting out pending machines. Chris drives around in a nice car, setting them up, collecting, and so on. She makes pretty good money.

I could be worse off. I could be all alone, no little baby loving me, no nice-looking girl like Chris bringing in the money. No nice meals and comfortable chair where I can sit all day and look at the river.

That was the way it was; that was what I was thinking when it happened. Chris came back from work early that day. She said she was taking little Will to the clinic for a checkup. Because of my condition, the local doctor had said little Will ought to have some tests to see if he'd inherited something. It meant an all-night stay, and she'd have to stay with him.

I'd miss the kid, but naturally I wanted him to be checked — not that he had inherited anything from *me*. But he had a slight cold. Maybe asthma. So I sat there bn the porch, watching the river as she bustled about packing things.

It was awful quiet in the house after they left. It was the first time I'd been alone since I came back. She'd set out some chow for me, so when the sunlight faded — a beautiful sunset over the river — I wheeled myself in. It was a wonderful meal, everything I liked. Nice, thin-cut cold ham and chicken, a tomato salad, cold corn muffins, and angel cake.

But there was something else, so I never ate that dinner. There was a note. Chris had left it tucked daintily against the sugar bowl. She had taken the kid and run off with Rogers to some unknown place where he had a "wonderful job." And she explained it all quite simply after saying she'd read this book after I'd failed to lock it up a few nights ago. "I ain't living with no big fat slob that calls *me ungrammatical.*"

She'd left the manuscript and Claire's letter which had been locked up with it; but in her preoccupation with greater things, like grammar, she hadn't taken the hint and had Rogers leave a gun on that table. There was no gas here now. But I could use a knife.

I never did use it. I don't even know if I tried. Dr.

Algee came calling some time later and found me unconscious on the kitchen floor. But I'm not so bad off now. I don't have to listen to that illiterate Chris, or that squalling brat of Walter Hunt's. True, I won't have anything more to write about. They say you lead an even life here; live longer than the poof sucker who has to work hard for a living. So I've got at least fifty years to look forward to.

I'm in a nice place. I have lots of friends around me. Men like myself, who did plenty for their country. Men who fought in Korea and in World War II. And plenty who were in the war before that. One man was even in the Spanish-American war. He was funny as hell telling about that, and then later about the French girls, the cognac and wine and all, in his next war.

Or he was funny for awhile. Until I cursed hell out of him, went into a screaming fit one day. I never saw him again. I guess they punished him for that. But it made it nice for me. They gave me a place of my own, where I can read Claire's letter out loud and not be laughed at by ignorant, unloved bastards like him. Because that's all I like to read now. I don't even look at pictures.

This vet hospital is in New York, but you'd never know it. I wouldn't, anyway, because I never look down at the streets or the rooftops. But they've fixed it so I can look out at the water. Yes, you can see the water and the boats from where I am, if you move close to the window so the bars make a nice frame.

You see lots of interesting things out there: the sun shining on the water, smoke from the whistles you can't hear till long after; sometimes big, handsome clouds. Even when it snows or rains, it's nice to watch from this snug place.

You don't see any clam-diggers, though. But hell, they're ignorant bastards. Why should I want to look at them? It makes me mad just to think of them. So mad that tears are running all over the paper right now.

THE END

# **Robert Ames Bibliography**
(1890-1991)

The Devil Drives (1952)
The Dangerous One (1954)
Awake and Die (1955)

As Charles L Clifford

*Novels*:
Too Many Boats (1934)
The Real Glory (1937)
While the Bells Rang (1941)
Sword of Allah (1941)

*Stories* (listed alphabetically):
Army Dog (*The Blue Book Magazine*, Nov 1941)
Army Girl (*Redbook Magazine*, Feb 1935)
Army Wife (*Redbook Magazine*, Oct 1937)
Beyond the Gate (*The Country Gentleman*, Nov 1940)
A Blaze of Glory (*Adventure*, Apr 1 1933)
The Brightest Bolo (*Adventure*, Jan 1 1931)
Broken Mirror (*Cosmopolitan*, Jan 1936)
Class Ring (*Argosy*, Aug 25 1934)
The Constabulary Comes Through (*Short Stories*, Oct 10 1931)
Contraband Rubies (*The Blue Book Magazine*, May 1947)
Danger Zone (*Adventure*, Sep 15 1932)
The Decoy (*Adventure*, July 1 1932)
Don Vincente's Treasure (*Argosy*, June 27 1931)
Eight Goal Men (*The Blue Book Magazine*, July 1935)
Far Call the Bugles (*The Blue Book Magazine*, Dec 1940)
Farewell Trumpet (*Argosy*, Oct 28 1939)
A Firl with a Line (*Redbook Magazine*, May 1940)
Follow the Guidon (*Collier's*, Oct 12 1940)
Hot Trail (*Adventure*, Apr 15 1932)
Hoyt of the Macabebes (*Adventure,* June 1 1931)
I Pledge Allegiance (*The Blue Book Magazine*, Dec 1946)

The Last Maneuvers (*Adventure*, Feb 1937)
Line of Duty (*The Blue Book Magazine*, June 1941)
A Long Chance at Linguasan (*Short Stories*, Nov 10 1931)
The Luck of the Scouts (*Short Stories*, Oct 10 1942)
Machine Gun Morale (*Adventure*, Sept 1 1931)
Mexican Lady (*Street & Smith's Complete Magazine*, Sept 1935)
More Vengeance in His Heart (*Short Stories*, Nov 25 1942)
One Hour to Wait (*The Saturday Evening Post*, Aug 6 1938)
One-Man Horse (*Adventure*, July 1933)
Over the Hill (*Adventure*, Oct 1 1930)
Parade Ground (*Redbook Magazine*, Feb 1934)
Philippine Incident (*Collier's*, Mar 21 1942)
Rank and File (with Mary C. McCall, Jr.; *Redbook Magazine*, Nov 1933)
The Real Glory (*Redbook Magazine*, Feb 1937)
Second Best Man (*Redbook Magazine*, Nov 1934)
The Second Chance (*Adventure*, Oct 1 1931)
The Stars Shine Bright (*The Blue Book Magazine*, Oct, Nov, Dec 1943)
The Sunshiner (*Adventure*, Nov 1 1930)
Sword of Allah (*Cosmopolitan*, May 1940)
They Never Die (*The Blue Book Magazine*, Nov 1949)
Two Kings of Love (*Redbook Magazine*, Dec 1934)
Two Men from Jolo (*Short Stories*, Aug 25 1931)
Typhoon Dawn (*The Blue Book Magazine*, July, Aug, Sep 1942)
War Chariot (*Redbook Magazine*, Feb 1940)
While the Bells Rang (*The American Magazine*, Mar 1941)
Word of Honor (*The Blue Book Magazine*, Jan 1951)

"Robert Ames" was born Charles Lee Clifford on October 23, 1890, in Boston, Massachusetts. He graduated from the U.S. Naval Academy in 1913 and later obtained a commission in the Army, rising to the rank of Colonel. While in the Army he trained Philippine troops prior to and during World War II, becoming Commanding Officer of the 2nd Filipino Infantry Regiment in 1942. Besides the three hardboiled novels he wrote for Gold Medal as Robert Ames, Clifford wrote several books and stories about the Philippines including *The Real Glory* (1937), filmed with Gary Cooper and David Niven in 1939. A veteran of both World wars, Clifford retired as a colonel in the Army after serving 32 years. He lived with his wife Elizabeth and three daughters in Tinton Falls since 1948, and died at age 100 on April 11, 1991, in Shrewsbury, New Jersey.

**Black Gat Books** is a new line of mass market paperbacks introduced in 2015 by Stark House Press. New titles appear every other month, featuring the best in crime fiction reprints. Each book is size to 4.25" x 7", just like they used to be, and priced at $9.99 (1–31) and $10.99 (32–). Collect them all.

- Harry Whittington · A Haven for the Damned #1 ·
- Charlie Stella · Eddie's World #2
- Leigh Brackett · Stranger at Home #3
- John Flagg · The Persian Cat #4
- Malcolm Braly · Felony Tank #6
- Vin Packer 8 The Girl on the Best Seller List #7
- Orrie Hitt · She Got What She Wanted #8
- Helen Nielsen · The Woman on the Roof #9
- Lou Cameron · Angel's Flight #10
- Gary Lovisi · The Affair of Lady Westcott's Lost Ruby / The Case of the Unseen Assassin #11
- Arnold Hano · The Last Notch #12
- Clifton Adams · Never Say No to a Killer #13
- Ed Lacy · The Men From the Boys #14
- Henry Kane · Frenzy of Evil #15
- William Ard · You'll Get Yours #16
- Bert & Dolores Hitchens · End of the Line #17
- Noël Calef · Frantic #18
- Ovid Demaris · The Hoods Take Over #19
- Fredric Brown · Madball #20
- Louis Malley Stool Pigeon #21
- Frank Kane · The Living End #22
- Ferguson Findley · My Old Man's Badge #23
- Paul Connolly · Tears are for Angels #24
- E. P. Fenwick · Two Names for Death #25
- Lorenz Heller · Dead Wrong #26
- Robert Martin · Little Sister #27
- Calvin Clements · Satan Takes the Helm #28
- Jack Karney · Cut Me In #29
- George Benet · The Hoodlums #30
- Jonathan Craig · So Young, So Wicked #31
- Edna Sherry · Tears for Jessie Hewitt #32
- William O'Farrell · Repeat Performance #33
- Marvin Albert · The Girl With No Place to Hide #34
- Edward S. Aarons · Gang Rumble #35
- William Fuller · Back Country #36
- Robert Silverberg · The Killer #37
- William R. Cox · Make My Coffin Strong #38
- A. S. Fleischman · Blood Alley #39
- Harold R. Daniels · The Girl in 304 #40
- William H. Duhart - The Deadly Pay-Off #41

**Stark House Press**
1315 H Street, Eureka, CA 95501 (707) 498-3135
griffinskye3@sbcglobal.net www.starkhousepress.com
Available from your local bookstore or direct from the publisher

www.ingramcontent.com/pod-product-compliance
Lightning Source LLC
LaVergne TN
LVHW021819060526
838201LV00058B/3446